definitely
COOL

Other Apple Paperbacks
you will enjoy:

Poor Girl, Rich Girl
by Johnniece Marshall Wilson

Sticks and Stones, Bobbie Bones
by Brenda Roberts

Once Upon a Time in Junior High
by Lisa Norment

Cousins
by Virginia Hamilton

definitely COOL

Brenda Wilkinson

AN
APPLE
PAPERBACK

SCHOLASTIC INC.
New York Toronto London Auckland Sydney

ISBN 0-590-43842-5

12 11 10 9 8 7 6 5 4 3 2 1   10   5 6 7 8 9/9 0/0

Printed in the U.S.A.   40

For my daughters, Kim and Lori

definitely
COOL

CHAPTER 1

So far, so good, Roxanne Williams thought, dressing for a morning she'd waited for so long — her first day of junior high!

The weatherman had said it was going to be in the seventies. Just right, she told herself. Not too hot, and not too cool. Now if I just don't look too preppy in this outfit, she thought as she stood looking into the mirror.

It was so like her, she realized, to find one thing to worry about after another. "You'd think I'd be satisfied knowing I wasn't going to be out of season!" she said out loud.

As a rule, Roxanne was a big worrier. But this morning was worse than ever! And last night had been just as bad. She'd tossed and turned all night, worrying about today. A new school. New people. New clothes. She wore a short plaid skirt, with matching knee socks and penny loafers, and an orange jacket.

"Smart," was her mother's description of this outfit, the first thing to catch her eye, as they walked

into the junior department of Macy's. Roxanne wasn't all that taken with it, but she had given in to her mother's wishes. And she was wearing the outfit *exactly* as the dummy had in the store. From top to bottom!

She only hoped that wasn't what she looked like in it. A big goofy dummy! She felt so tall — *too* tall to only be going into seventh grade! She'd experienced many an embarrassing moment because of her height. Rather than argue with the token booth collector, her mother started paying subway fare for her long before Roxanne's time. Then just last week, a new lady in the projects tried to guess what grade she was in, and placed her all the way in high school! Her mother had tried to clean it up, by saying that the lady probably couldn't see too well at her age. But Roxanne didn't buy it. She felt sure the old lady saw her shooting up to the sky the same as everybody else could.

"Daaag," she mumbled at her reflection now. I sure hope kids meeting me for the first time don't get the wrong impression. Seeing the giant I am, they may think I'm repeating a grade or something! And I'd just die over that — somebody thinking I'm dumb! Not that I'm a genius or anything like that. But I *am* most definitely in the right grade!

"Roxanne!" her mother was calling out now. "We're going to be late."

"We?" she asked, heading straight to her mother's room to clear this up.

"Chile, what in harm's creation have you gone and done to your eyebrows?" her mother fired, the minute she saw her. "You look silly!"

Roxanne squirmed as she reached up to touch the slanted spaces she'd made in each brow. It was a new *exotic* look she had seen in *Essential* magazine. And so she tried to explain.

"*Essential* says that this is the new *hot* look for the black woman," she began, only to be cut off by her mother's famous dry tone — the voice she used to say something was ridiculous.

"You happen to be the black *girl!*" her mother broke in on her. "And hot, your brows are not!"

"I just wanted to try something different," Roxanne said pitifully. Then moving closer to the mirror, she checked to see if she looked as tacky as her mother was making out. One brow *was* a little crooked, but the total look wasn't *that* ragged. At least it wasn't to *her*! So she tried to do like the song says — "Fight the power!"

"Why every time I try something new you have to knock it?" she asked her mother.

"That's not true," her mother replied.

"You told me my hairstyle looked *ghettoish* the other day."

"Well, baby, it *didn't* look nice," her mother in-

3

sisted. "I don't want you going out in the street with your hair plastered down on the sides like I see some young girls — a slick halo of grease shining around the side of their cute, little faces. I'm sure their mothers don't catch them leaving that way, because they'd tell them better, too!"

"Cheese and crackers!" Roxanne mumbled under her breath. "There she goes speaking for every-body's mother now!"

"I remember when you put those extra holes in your ears without my permission," her mother con-tinued. "Now this. No telling what you're subject to try next!"

"Oh, Mommie," Roxanne groaned, truly exasper-ated. She couldn't believe her mother was ag-gravating her like this — bad as her nerves were already!

Then suddenly, as though she could read her mind, her mother turned sweet. "We really should be moving, baby," she said softly.

"That's what I came in here to ask you about!" Roxanne told her. "You say *we*! I don't need you to go with me, you know!"

"Well, I wasn't sure," her mother began. "I thought maybe you'd want me to come with you part of the way. Maybe walk you to the bus stop."

"No way!" cried Roxanne. "Everybody'll be standing there. I can't believe you thought I wanted you to escort me!"

"You did every year up until now," she was reminded.

"But it's *junior high*, Mommie!" Roxanne stressed. "People would think I'm stupid-crazy if I came bopping up to school with my *mother*!"

"Enough said," her mother announced with a brisk brush of the hands. "It's settled. I can go straight to work from now on!"

"Yes, you can," Roxanne sang out, turning and doing a little dip as she spoke. Then spreading her arms and posing like a model, she rapped, "How-you-like-me-now?"

"Just gorgeous. Just gorgeous. But stop slumping," her mother ordered the minute Roxanne went into a slouched position. "You're a tall girl, so *be* tall! You really are beautiful," she came closer to say. Then pinching her daughter's cheek, she cracked, "Beautiful, minus those way-out eyebrows!"

"Yea, yea," Roxanne uttered, making a funny face.

"Nay, nay," her mother came back with, silly face and all.

They had fun together at times like this. And Roxanne never wanted them to end — with her mother being her mother, her mother being her friend.

"You know, Mommie, these *are* my eyes," she kidded, about to leave the room.

"And you *are* my child! And hear me clearly, C-H-I-L-D!" her mother spelled out. "Even if you are headed for junior high! So no more mutilating yourself without my permission!"

"Mommie, how can you call shaving my eyebrows mutilation?" she questioned, laughing.

"I'm including the extra holes you went and put in your ears, chopping off your hair without my permission, and any other such act!"

"Okay, okay. You win!" Roxanne said. Then she left the room to get her things.

When she returned, all ready to leave, her mother was standing by the doorway. And she had on her face, what Roxanne called The Special! It was a wide-eyed, crazy smile of adoration that Roxanne felt could only come to a child from a parent. Or maybe a grandparent or some other such *adorer*! she had considered. She had seen lots of folks giving The Special to children. They'd stand looking at the particular child like they were the most fabulous creature on earth!

Now while she wouldn't deny being fairly cute, Roxanne knew that no one could be as gorgeous as her mother made her feel, smiling at her the way she was doing now! She knew better than to let it go to her head though. It was perfectly clear to her that this was just mother love.

Unable, it seemed, to keep her hands off her this morning, her mother patted her on the shoulder a final time as she headed out the door. Then kissing her good-bye, she chanted, "You're sharp, Roxanne. Real sharp!"

"It's *fresh*, Mommie," Roxanne tried schooling her for what seemed like the *umpteenth* time. "Fresh! People were sharp in the olden days. In the nineties *we be fresh!*"

"I want you *to be* dropping that bad grammar as soon as you hit the classroom," Mrs. Williams reminded her.

"For suuure," Roxanne crooned, knowing how this line got on her mother's nerves, too.

"That outfit's *saying something*!" were her mother's last words.

Saying something? Roxanne thought, smiling and shaking her head as she walked to the elevator. There's just no hope. I'm never going to rid Mommie of her ole timey expressions!

Aimlessly, she ran her hand along the hallway wall. Painted a bright yellow with tiny orange flowers, the hallways were a real eyesore. Roxanne liked the old color much better. Until recently, the walls were light green and the doors a darker shade. While they were painting the halls orange and yellow, Roxanne had wondered what color they had in mind for the doors. Orange? Or yellow? Either would have been outrageous, she figured. So she was relieved when they left the doors green. Not that she liked it. It would have been nice, she thought, if the housing authority had made the doors a nice sensible brown. But housing wasn't for going out of their way. They gave you few choices when you lived in the projects. Inside, every apartment was painted white, beige, or green. And the hallways in every building were the same loud yellow and orange.

Some tenants tried to add a little something different on their floor like a painting or a fake plant. Tenants on Roxanne's floor had put money together for a mirror made up of squares. It looked nice when it first went up, all bordered off with wood. But lately, kids had been breaking the mirror squares one by one. Mrs. Edwards, who lived next door to Roxanne, kept replacing the broken squares. The mirror held sentimental value to her. Her late husband had tacked up the wooden border. So keeping the mirror in place, Mrs. Edwards said, was like keeping a little piece of him alive.

As Roxanne passed the mirror now, she got a final glimpse of herself. Looking back to where her mother stood in the doorway, she shouted, "This definite cool potential!"

"Definite cool potential?" her mother, mocked her. Then dropping to the dry tone once more, she warned, "Don't walk out of here with that crazy talk and vain thought!"

"Oh, I'm only fooling," Roxanne confessed. "I'm about as nervous as a chick coming out the shell!"

"I can still come with you," her mother offered, like it hadn't sunk in that this was the last thing Roxanne wanted! The elevator came, saving her from having to repeat it.

"Look for Rolland and other people you know already!" her mother was shouting as Roxanne let the elevator door slam. Rolland? she groaned, falling up against the wall of the empty elevator. I'm trying to make progress. Rolland, and anybody else I graduated with from P.S. 9, are the *last* people I want to hook up with in junior high!

CHAPTER 2

Wouldn't you know whose face would be the first Roxanne saw on the bus line? *Rolland's!*

Here she was trying to look sophisticated and grown-up, like it wasn't the first time she was riding the city bus to school. And Rolland was jumping up and down calling out her name and waving, like they were two little kids starting kindergarten! The worst part of it for her was that some cute guys were at the bus stop. One or two of them kind of looking out the side of their eyes, like maybe they were curious about who she was!

And here's Rolland Palmer Jones Reese with his longname self, sweatin' me! she thought. Just please don't let anybody think I'm his girlfriend. Or that he's anyone that special to me!

Rolland, with the many last names, lived in the same building of the projects as Roxanne. Along with this, the two had been in the same class since nursery school. It wouldn't have been so bad if Rolland's "moms" (as he called her) had taught him the importance of not wearing out his welcome at somebody else's house! It was a lesson Roxanne's mother gave her early on.

But Rolland's mom was a Mary Kay cosmetic lady — one always on the go.

She'd been married three or four times, which Roxanne figured was the lady's business. But it was *everybody's* business, thanks to her son, who insisted on tacking on each new name! No one could convince him what a nuisance it was to hear a teacher rambling through all those names for roll call year after year!

The youngest in a kind of mixed-up family, Rolland longed for attention. And Roxanne realized that the name thing was one way of him getting it!

Far back as she could remember, he had said he liked her. She had gone along with it when she was little, but said "no thanks" to the girl-friend/boyfriend business later on. At the present time, Rolland was just a friend who lived downstairs. No matter how much he liked pretending otherwise.

Like he's doing now! she was thinking. He's forever singing, "Roxanne and Rolland," and saying how gooood our names sound together! Just *thinking* about him saying it, grosses me out!

She stepped back from in line, to put more space between them.

"What's wrong?" Rolland asked, a worried look coming over his face.

"Nothing!" she mumbled. "I just want the bus to come."

As much as the boy got on her nerves, Roxanne could never out-and-out hurt his feelings! They went back together too far to do something like that.

When they were little, he would come up to her house and practically take over every toy she owned! And in turn, she got to play with his toys. Between them they had the best of it all.

But then Roxanne started getting tired of Rolland. She got sick of him ringing her bell going, "Whatcha doin', Rox-aanne?" followed with, "Whatcha got good ta eaaat?"

With his moms always traveling, and his older brothers not halfway wanting to be bothered with him, Rolland was always scouting around for some-place to be. And nine times out of ten, it was at Roxanne's in 7C. He used to eat with her almost every day. But he finally chilled on that.

The same way Roxanne grew up and got embar-rassed over being called his girlfriend, he began to feel funny about coming for supper every night. But when he was too little to know anything about shame, Rolland was a regular at suppertime!

Roxanne worried that it was her joking him about

it one evening that made him stop coming. She had kidded that he must have been able to smell her mother's pots from downstairs! She noticed that Rolland cooled off shortly afterward. And from then on, whenever she looked out the window at a certain time in the evening, she could see him coming into the building with a greasy bag from the fish fry place or the Chinese restaurant. If not from there, from Mickey D's, Popeye's, or someplace like that. Roxanne couldn't help feeling sorry for him.

All and all he's not *too* bad! she thought now, looking at him and smiling to herself. I do have some pretty good memories of times with ole knucklehead! She used the name she called him when they fought as little children. Not that they fought often. And he didn't let anybody else bother her, either! Rolland would take up for Roxanne like a real brother in the playground. Before he claimed her as a girlfriend, he told people they were cousins. He was pretty funny as a little boy.

Roxanne still snapped on him sometimes about how he used to rush up to her house Christmas morning, asking if Santa Claus had brought her baby-that-a-way, baby-tender-love, or whatever the hot doll of the season was. After seeing the thing advertised on TV from Thanksgiving on, Rolland would be dying to play with the doll as much as she was! Of course he wasn't about to ask for one of his own. But he couldn't wait to get his little hands on hers!

She had such fun teasing him about the past. Rolland would try to deny the stories. But Roxanne would say, "Just 'fess up, because you know it's all the gospel truth!"

She remembered now how Rolland had tried to pass her a love note in third grade one day. It read: "Dear Roxanne, I love you very much." And at the bottom, he had signed in his scribbly writing (with the letters all running together) "ASHY BOY," instead of "A Shy Boy!" like he meant.

And who ended up snatching the note, but ole crazy Boobie Watson! she recalled. Boobie passed the note around for everybody to see! And both Rolland and Roxanne were ragged for days. Rolland was teased for writing it. And poor Roxanne, for being the one he was sending the stupid thing to!

It was only when something embarrassing happened to somebody else in class, that people got off their backs. It was the only way she remembered kids at P.S. 9 *ever* stopped jiving a person over something embarrassing! You had to wait until something as terrible or worse happened to somebody else.

The bus was there at last. As Roxanne had stood, lost in her private thoughts, Rolland had rambled on endlessly about his summer vacation in South Carolina. He had only gotten back yesterday.

"Nice outfit," Rolland complimented Roxanne, as they stepped up on the bus.

"Thanks," she said. Noticing that what he was wearing wasn't bad either, she thought she'd be nice and say so.

But no sooner had she spoken than she wondered, What did I want to go and do that for? The boy was smiling wider than Arsenio Hall!

He really did look together though, she thought as they rode on. Seems like he may have improved a little in the looks department over the summer, too, she told herself, continuing to check him out. His skin's a smoother darker brown. Voice sounds a lil' deeper. But he still ain't saying nothing! she decided as he babbled on and on.

"What time you plan to leave each morning?" Rolland eased off his summer vacation speech to ask.

Roxanne looked out the window, trying to pretend she hadn't heard him.

"I say what time you leaving every day, Roxanne?" he repeated, nudging her in the side this time.

"Oh! Oh!" she stammered. "Ah-I-I'm probably gonna leave 'roun' eight-something."

And even as she gave him half an answer, she was thinking, Whatever it takes, I'm finding some

15

way to miss this boy in the morning!

"Maybe we'll be lucky like before, and end up in the same homeroom," he said next, as though his dreams were her own.

"Rolland, junior high's a place where you get to stretch out — where you meet *new* people!" she told him. "Don't you understand?"

Without a word about it, he went right back to his summer vacation. A mall had opened up in South Carolina where his grandmother lived. And he was sounding off, like somebody just back from Disney World!

She had stopped him earlier to say that *she'd* been to a mall before — one right up in Westchester, not far from where they lived in the Bronx. But that didn't shut him up! The boy was on a roll!

"It's like an all-day party!" he was saying now. "There are groups of guys, girls. You can go see a movie, play video games. EAT! And, oh, the good food they have down South."

"Of which I guess you had your share and somebody else's!" she kidded, poking him in the side.

"Oh, I can't help myself down there!" he declared. "Food don't even taste the same way! Ice cream. Cake. Doughnuts. Everything sweet here, taste sweeter there. And my grandmother cooks vegetables *straight* from her garden. Fresh stuff! You know how I be saying I don't like tomatoes? Well, I do down there. I like them mixed with corn and okra!"

"Oooh, *okra*!" Roxanne groaned, frowning and making a face. "Who could like that slimy stuff?"

"I did. And any other kind of vegetables my grandmother cooked! I know my stomach was going, 'Ohh! Ahh! What's this? What's that?' he joked.

"You're wack!" she said, cracking up along with him, until they suddenly had to turn and see just what was going on in the back of the bus. There had been a lot of noise there all along. But now, a group of kids was *really* carrying on!

"They must think they're outside," Rolland commented on the three girls sitting on the backseat causing the commotion.

"Yeah," Roxanne agreed. "Back there 'just performing,' as my mother would say." She shook her head.

Meanwhile the girls kept it up, hitting at one another, and screaming and falling onto the floor.

Roxanne noticed that they all had on the kind of big gold loop earrings, she'd been dying to own. She remembered now, that the earrings were one more thing her mother had dissed! When she first mentioned wanting a pair, she had pointed them out to her mother on a girl wearing two sets in each ear.

"No way!" her mother cried. "I'm not about to let you go walking around with those doorknockers on your ears!" And she'd added that they looked too womanish on girls.

Seeing them now on the three loud girls in back, Roxanne wondered if maybe her mother hadn't been right. The things do look right grown! she thought, studying them.

"Hey, *you!*" one of the girls called out all of a sudden, looking dead at Roxanne. "You in the orange jacket! You lose som'thin' back here or som'thin'?"

"I-I," Roxanne stammered, totally confused by this attack.

"Just turn around, turn around!" Rolland said quickly, sounding like he had to protect her. "Act like you didn't hear her — like you don't even see them back there!"

"Why she breaking on me like that?" Roxanne asked, looking puzzled. "I'm not the only person who looked at them."

"But you were staring," Rolland explained. "Some people don't like you staring. My brother say the best thing to do out here, is to look straight ahead. Comin' and goin'. That way you don't risk being misunderstood. Too many people are jumpy. Anything can set 'em off!"

"And some, I guess are just troublemakers from the git-go!" Roxanne added.

"Wooord," he said.

"So junior high means looking in the sky!" she cracked.

"And eating a lil' humble pie!" Rolland threw in. "There was no point in your getting into it with that group in back. Just let what the girl said fly. Because I hear some crazy things happen on these buses!"

"You don't have to tell me," Roxanne said. "My father drives a bus, remember!"

"So you should know the score! Look around," Rolland continued. "Even the grown people on here, acting like they don't see those girls. And the driver? He's probably just hoping they don't try anything too stupid before he reaches the school stop!"

"In the first place I'm not wearing any orange!" Roxanne pointed out. "The girl doesn't know rust from orange!"

"Just forget it!" Rolland said. "What difference does it make? Orange? Rind?"

"I said *rust*!" she corrected him. "Not rind, boy! Besides. Whoever heard of the color rind?"

"Whoever heard of rust?" he asked.

"Rust," Roxanne stated, "is the color between orange and brown! The color of fall leaves!"

"Rind!" he insisted still.

"Like what?" Roxanne questioned.

"Like — like the watermelon rind!" he joked.

"Git outta here," she said, shoving at him.

"Well rust or orange," Rolland repeated, "it still

don't matter. The color I'm concerned about is black and blue. Which is how you could end up, getting into it with that group!" he said, nodding his head in the direction of the girls still acting up in back.

"Hmph!" Roxanne huffed, trying to sound bad. "They just better not play *me*, 'cause I ain't the lotto!"

The bus made a sharp swing and headed up a hill. They were in Riverdale now.

For years Roxanne had looked from her bedroom window at the trees and tall buildings that stood at a distance in Riverdale. They seemed so close, but so far. Though she lived but what was said to be "a skip and a hop away," she never had cause to come to Riverdale before today.

Roxanne always wondered if it was as ritzy up here as people said. Seems like it is, she thought, as the bus rolled past one well-kept building after another.

Even the names of the buildings sounded rich! The Regency. Royal Oaks. Grandview! THE WHITE-HALL, read the carving on a grayish-looking building. Probably more like the white ALL! Roxanne joked to herself. She figured that was about all who lived there! But no. Wait a minute! she had to back up and say, as a black man and woman came from The Whitehall. Must be lawyers, or doctors, or somebody important, she was thinking. Who else could afford to be up here livin' large? Tennis courts. Swimming pools . . .

With everything looking as nice as it did outside the buildings, Roxanne could only imagine how fabulous the apartments must be inside!

Not that there's anything wrong with the inside of where I live, she told herself. Her mother had their apartment fixed up nice. It's outside the projects that's so gross! she thought with disgust.

The first thing you saw when you walked in the projects was paper and other windblown junk all scattered! Then there were the broken-down benches in front of the buildings. And the cheap front doors all scratched up with curses and stupid people's names.

What Roxanne hated most of all, were the big, stinking garbage bins outside each building of the projects! Something she didn't see anywhere in Riverdale!

The outside garbage bins were supposed to help the environment! While she was as much for saving the planet as the next person, she wished people in the projects could make their contribution some way other than those stinking bins! The trash used to get burned in the incinerator, but the city stopped that. Now everything got dumped outside to be picked up.

She figured the people who decided on this knew

what they were doing. Not burning garbage obviously *did* make the air cleaner. But she wondered why the *geniuses* never stopped to think about how it was going to smell around the projects. Not to mention what the open garbage drew! Drug people digging for empty cans and bottles to sell. Rats.

"Check out that limousine!" Rolland shouted, pulling her away from her thoughts. "Must be one of those politicians they say live in Riverdale! It's another world up here, ain't it, Roxie?"

"Wooord," she uttered, still gazing at everything they passed.

When they finally reached Riverdale Junior High, she could see that Rolland had read the bus driver right. The man was smiling as the school kids got off his bus.

She was so busy watching the driver that she didn't notice what was happening behind her. One of the Doorknockers had fallen into her on purpose. Or so she thought, from how the girl laughed and said, *"Excuse me!"* afterward.

Roxanne wanted to say something. But since she couldn't *prove* that the girl had fallen into her deliberately, she let the whole thing slide.

CHAPTER 3

A rainbow of seventh-graders were spread out in the auditorium. This was where they had been told to report, once they reached school. Roxanne stood by the door checking out the scene. Seeing that she wasn't about to lose Ashy Boy, she told him she was going to the rest room.

"I'll wait here for you," Rolland said, freezing on the spot.

"No! You go on," she insisted, going so far as to give him a little push. "Go on and find yourself a seat. You don't need to wait for me."

On her own at last, she went down the hallway, walking like she'd been around awhile! She had taken no more than a step or two, when a boy singled her out laughing. "Check out those zebra brows!" he shouted, pointing her out to what she took to be his posse. The whole group was laughing at her now.

With her head lowered, Roxanne flew to the rest room! As soon as she got inside, she got busy filling in the shaven spaces in her brows with a pen.

A girl stood next to her in the mirror putting a lot of makeup on her face, and dirtying up the sink. It was too much goo for school. Too much mess for anywhere! Roxanne told herself, trying her best not to stare. With the makeup spread all outside her eyes, the girl looked like Morticia from *The Addams Family*! Roxanne was so tickled, she almost forgot being laughed at herself a few minutes before.

When she'd first stepped up to the mirror, she had been concerned about the girl seeing that she was using a ballpoint pen for an eyebrow pencil. But she could tell now that there was no need to worry. Because Morticia's not thinking about a soul in this mirror except herself! she joked, hurrying to finish.

She didn't want anybody else to walk in and take her for a makeup queen, too. Roxanne made up her mind here to never try anything like this again! She was going to be natural from now on. No *exotic* eyes, no extra nothing after today! she decided.

Her brows weren't perfect, but she'd managed to get them pretty close to normal. Normal enough to walk back down the hall without getting ragged, she hoped, as she left the rest room. On her way back to the auditorium, another guy called out to her.

"Yo, light skin, walk this way!" he said grinning stupidly.

What kind of simple garbage is he talking? Roxanne wondered. Pointing out somebody that way! *Light skin?* I never heard of anything so stupid. Daag! Here I came to junior high, expecting people to be grown-up. Well I'm sure not impressed so far. Nobody ever called me a color name at P.S. 9!

Though she'd had no intention of looking for Rolland before, her hallway run-ins had her scouting out his familiar face now. Her eyes roamed the auditorium like a lost baby's in a department store.

"Roxanne! Over here," she heard him calling from the center of the room. She relaxed once she flopped down beside Rolland.

"Why you change your eyebrows?" he came out with, to her surprise. And before she could answer, he told her that he thought they were fly.

"You really like them?" she asked. "I didn't know you even noticed. You never said anything."

"Don't mean I didn't peep it," he said, working his shoulders with the words. "I see a whole lot that I don't speak on, Roxanne," he continued. "It so happens that I do know what time it is! You just won't ever give me credit. But as for the young ladies down South . . ."

"Okay, Rolland," she said. "You deep. You know what's up. Where it's at!" she ended, laughing and patting him on the back.

"Git outta here," he said, shoving her hand away,

but clearly enjoying her fussing over him.

"We better chill and pay attention to what's going on," Roxanne stopped teasing him to say. "We may miss our names being called."

Looking around the auditorium, she checked to see how many people from their elementary school had come to Riverdale Junior High. Most had come here. But some, like her number-one homegirl, Maxine, had gone on to other junior high schools. Maxine was from the projects, too. And the girl was, as Roxanne put it, "like major smart!"

Maxine had told her how bored she got in class sometimes, sitting waiting for everyone else to catch on. Teachers never had to go over anything but once with her. One time she'd even corrected a teacher! It was a math problem that the teacher had added wrong on the board. The teacher turned a little red, but had to give Maxine credit for being right. Mouths were hanging half-opened the rest of the afternoon. But Maxine told Roxanne afterward, that it was no big deal. Teachers were human, too, she said. And they had just as much a right to make a mistake sometime as anybody else did.

The Max, as Roxanne sometimes called her best friend, made straight EXCELLENTS all through elementary school! Roxanne had wanted so much for the two of them to stay together forever. And so had Maxine. But they learned at graduation that Maxine had a full scholarship to a private school in Riverdale.

"I guess those are just the breaks," Roxanne had said to her mother when she shared her mixed feelings about the situation. She was glad for Maxine, but sad for their friendship. She knew that they could still be together around the projects and everything, but it would never be the same. Because, as she'd explained to her mother, and was thinking right now, *Everybody needed a main homegirl at school!*

She had been friendly with other girls from P.S. 9 — but only so-so. So-so, meaning that she spoke to other girls and played games with them in the school yard. But Roxanne never truly hung with any girl but Maxine, at school or around the projects. So she was pretty much out there on her own in seventh grade, hoping to hook up with somebody new.

One or two girls that she was so-so with kind of half-smiled when she caught their eye in the auditorium. They didn't seem to mind letting on that they knew her from elementary school. But others quickly turned their heads away. Roxanne wasn't taking this hard though, because she understood. Like them, she, too, was looking for new faces to connect with. And not just the same-o same-o.

As teachers continued calling out names, she noticed what a racial mix of people there was in seventh grade. Everybody can be satisfied that they had someone like them, she figured.

It hadn't always been that way at P.S. 9. What made her think of this now was hearing Kiku Kam's name called. A Vietnamese girl, Kiku had been the only Asian girl at P.S. 9 from first to third grade. It had been hard for her to fit in with American girls at first. Roxanne used to pull her into games in the school yard. Little by little Kiku learned how to play hopscotch and do all the hand games American girls played. And Kiku taught *them* things, like how to use chopsticks. Roxanne smiled to herself, remembering how she demonstrated for them with two pencils.

In the beginning some kids complained that it was hard to understand what Kiku was saying when she talked. But Roxanne wasn't about to hold that against a person. For she'd known people to say that they couldn't understand some of what *she* was saying — when all the while she felt she was speaking perfectly good English!

She simply learned to listen closely when Kiku spoke — the only thing it took to understand someone who sounded a little different.

Kiku caught her eye as she returned now from getting her placement card.

"Roxanne!" she called out, in the soft voice that

always sounded like somebody singing. "I'm in 7A. Maybe you'll get the same, yes?"

"Sounds good to me," Roxanne responded, making her giggle — because this was Kiku's own famous last line, "Sounds good to me."

They had called Rolland's name now. As he grinned over new kids laughing at his long last name, Roxanne slid down into her seat and turned around like she didn't know him.

Before joining his assigned group, Rolland stopped to tell her he'd been assigned to 7C.

"Okay," she said. "You better go on." After he left, she thought, 7A, B, E, or D will be fine for me!

CHAPTER 4

Not only was Rolland not in Roxanne's homeroom, but few from P.S. 9 were. Besides Kiku, there were only Lisa Brody and Jessica Fine, both of whom she was only so-so with. Roxanne had known Lisa and Jessica since kindergarten. But she didn't feel close enough to them to go and plant herself in the middle of the group they'd formed with two other girls. Kiku, she'd at least spoken to today. But this didn't give her courage to go and plop herself in the group Kiku was sitting with either.

So Roxanne sat alone, trying all the while to keep an expression on her face that said she didn't mind being by herself.

Looking around the room, she studied what was happening. As much as she could understand people wanting to be around someone *just* like them, she felt it was kind of a shame how everybody grouped off. Black and black sat together. White and white. The same with Hispanics. Asians. Everybody had a clique!

Just like it was the last two years at P.S. 9, she

couldn't help thinking. They had all started out mixing together in kindergarten. Then year by year they ended up in these different racial groups. It had happened at P.S. 9, and she could tell it was going to be pretty much the same here in junior high.

About the only place in the room where this wasn't taking place was in the back. A dozen people sat there — just as it had been in elementary school.

At P.S. 9, there was always a group of troublemakers who sat as far away from the teacher as they could get. Also in the back, was what Roxanne saw as "shy people." Shy, she sensed, over not having on the so-called right sneakers, the latest fashions, and junk like that.

She felt bad for kids who sat in the back because they felt that they weren't dressed right. Some kids had parents who refused to go along with buying them high-priced sneakers and other things kids in the front of the room wore. Others just didn't have the money. Not that parents of many up-front people (including her own) had a lot of money.

Roxanne knew for sure that many kids at P.S. 9 wearing the latest, weren't much better off financially than some in back. But somehow they all managed to beg their folks into getting them what they wanted.

Her own mother stayed on her, telling her that it was ridiculous to want something just because everybody else had it. But still, she gave in a lot. Roxanne knew that her mother had her limits though. Like the eighty-dollar sneakers that The Max got for school. Roxanne told Maxine that she knew not to even try it with her mother!

She had worked her mother for all she could though, when they'd gone school shopping the week before. But she'd had no luck in breaking her down for the main thing she wanted! It was a jean jacket that she told Maxine was too 'live for her to even describe. Then she'd gone on and done exactly that! She also told how she'd pleaded with her mother to buy the jacket.

"After begging and begging my mother, I made out like a rapper," she said to Maxine. "I sang, 'Mommie, you gotta be cool, while you're in school! You hafta look 'live to survive! You need to be fly to get by! You gotta dress hot to stay on top!' And, girl, my mother laughed, but never moved one inch closer to buying me that jacket!"

As the homeroom teacher, Mrs. Weisbaum, called up different students to give them schedule information, Roxanne sized up this year's back-of-the-room crowd. One boy, Nelson, was already being given a new name by boys in the back. Once Nelson spoke, you could hear a southern sound in his voice. And he kept going, "Yes, ma'am," as he answered

Mrs. Weisbaum, instead of plain "yes" like everybody else had done.

"Countrytime," Roxanne heard them tag him, naming the poor boy after a soft drink. Nelson laughed, too, surviving the best he could in back. Somebody was already imitating how he sounded when he spoke. Roxanne sat pitying him, until she caught herself.

Who am *I* to be feeling sorry for anyone? she thought. Still sitting here by myself. Even having Rolland to talk with would be better than this!

She wondered what Rolland was doing now. She couldn't believe her eyes earlier, when she saw him leaving the auditorium talking to a girl! And a pretty one at that! she recalled. He had been standing in line next to the girl, along with the rest of the people in his homeroom group. Roxanne had glanced over and checked out the two chitchatting. Then the next thing she knew they had taken off alone. All she could do was utter, "Hmph! Hmph! Hmph!" Rolland! Of all people to meet somebody new the first day!

It would be a shame if I don't get to meet at least *one* new person, she told herself now. Girl or guy, it doesn't matter. As long as I have *something* to report back to The Max! I bet she'll meet some really rich kids, instead of a few semirich ones like there seem to be here. I'm sure I'll meet other kids at lunchtime. Someone other than the seventh-grade babies sitting here, she tried convincing herself, as she looked around a room where there were so many who looked younger than she. Roxanne slid down in her seat now, trying to look shorter.

She couldn't help noticing the one black girl and one white girl huddled up in back, laughing and talking with each other.

Wonder if they know each other from before? she questioned. Or could they have just hit if off right away?

They didn't look like cutups, who sat in the back. They *were* dressed sort of plain though, wearing regular sweat suits and sneakers. But they weren't back there looking unnecessary, like the average shy person tended to do.

If the two girls felt in any way funny about their outfits, it certainly wasn't showing! They looked as comfortable with themselves as anybody up front! I haven't got a category for the two of *them*! she thought. That was how *she* wanted to be known in junior high. As someone *undescribable*!

She felt that she wasn't getting off to a good start though. But then she thought, maybe. Maybe people *didn't know* just what to make of her, sitting there by herself looking stupid!

One group of girls near her looked pretty cool. Roxanne longed like crazy to move two seats over and join them, but was too scared to try. She worried that they wouldn't want another person. So instead of checking it out, she opened her notebook and began doodling to be busy.

She thought how different it had been the first day of elementary school. You simply walked up to people and made friends! You never stopped to wonder whether someone liked you or not. You just figured the whole world loved you. Because that was pretty much how you felt about the whole world! Maybe that was why it was so easy for all of us to mix way back then, she considered.

She saw Lisa and Jessica looking her way now. But since neither one motioned for her to come sit with them, Roxanne stayed put. It was almost time to go anyhow. She'd made it up to now, so she figured she could get through the rest of the time they had left there.

As they were leaving for first period, one of the girls from the group she had longed to join came walking toward her. Roxanne's heart thumped with excitement. At last, she thought. Somebody knows I'm alive!

"Why were you sitting in homeroom not talking to anybody like that?" the girl asked.

Right away Roxanne noticed that she wasn't African-American, like she'd thought. The girl's skin was browner than her own, but her accent made

Roxanne think that she was Hispanic, Panamanian, or something like that.

"I hardly knew anybody in homeroom," Roxanne explained. "Only three other people in the class come from the same elementary school . . ."

"You think I knew the girls I was talking with?" she asked. And Roxanne admitted that she had.

"No more than I know you!" she informed her. Then smiling, the girl introduced herself. "I'm Margarita. You're . . . ?"

"Roxanne."

"Well maybe I'll see you around later," Margarita said, starting off in another direction.

Shoot! thought Roxanne. Why couldn't we be going the same way? She was alone again. But at least now she had someone to tell Maxine she'd met — a new girl named Margarita!

CHAPTER 5

Roxanne found herself at lunchtime, standing in a pay phone calling her mother at work! She knew this was *pitiful*. But it was all she could think of to do!

Everybody seemed to have somewhere to go or somebody to talk to. She had been unable to connect with anyone in the two classes she'd been in so far. She'd desperately hoped to be able to hook up with Margarita during lunch period, but the girl was nowhere to be seen! And as far as Roxanne meeting anybody new in the cafeteria (like she dreamed about earlier) forget it! She was worse off there than she'd been in homeroom. At least in the classroom, she'd been able to hide behind a book. But in the cafeteria she was wide open for all to see.

She had stood up front, holding her tray and staring like there was someone definite she was looking for. She'd frowned and strained her eyes, making all kinds of faces, as if to say her "person" just wasn't there! As her eyes circled the cafeteria, she had spotted Rolland! Then just as she was about to join him, who came up from behind her but the *girl* — the same one Rolland had left the auditorium with that morning! And the girl headed straight his way!

Roxanne had thought of trying to play it off cool, and walk on over and join the two of them. But when she saw Rolland pull out a chair for the girl, like they were a special twosome, she lost all heart!

Seeing an empty space in the corner of the cafeteria, she hurried and grabbed it. As she choked down her lunch, she figured if anybody from homeroom saw her, they surely had her marked as hopeless. First, no friends in morning homeroom. Then, none at lunch! One long tall *zero*! was how she saw herself. And everyone else must, too! she decided. So, eating as quickly as she could, she finished and got out of the cafeteria!

And it was here in the phone booth that she'd escaped.

"Hello, Mommie," she said.

"Everything all right, sweetie?" her mother asked.

"Yeah." Roxanne tried to pretend at first, but then broke down and got real. "It's just that it's lunchtime. And I don't really know anybody. Well, I met *one* girl. But I didn't see her in the cafeteria and I couldn't find a soul to eat with. So I rushed through my food and left!"

"Well, baby, why don't you try going to the library?" her mother suggested.

"Oh, suuuure!" Roxanne crooned. "The library. Where all the excitement's happening the first day!"

"Well, it was just a thought," said her mother. "What about Rolland?"

"We're in different classes," said an impatient Roxanne. "Besides, I'm trying to get to know *new* people!"

"Well, it certainly won't happen inside a phone booth," her mother teased.

"Mommie, this isn't funny!" she cried. "I'm serious."

"I know, baby," she said. "I know it's scary."

"I'm dying out here," Roxanne confessed. "You just don't know. A stupid boy called out, 'Hey, light skin!' to me."

"Who? What?" Her mother jumped right in.

Roxanne asked if she had ever heard of anything like it before.

"Not that. But something similar," her mother explained. "Redbones was the expression of my time. It would hurt when I was called that. Like I gather you were. The boy probably thought he was flattering you. People can say ignorant things about skin color sometimes. So what you have to do is learn how to ignore such foolish remarks. Color doesn't matter. It's what's inside that counts."

Roxanne laughed. She reminded her mother that this was the very same line she'd used the other day, in refusing to buy her the jean jacket. "That it's what's inside that counts."

"Well, it holds true for so much, sweetie," her mother stated. "You carried on like your life depended on that overpriced dungaree jacket!" she said, breaking Roxanne's dream jacket down to the very ordinary *dungarees*. "All the hundred-dollar jackets in the world can't make someone better, baby! It's not what's on someone's back that counts. And also, dark skin, light skin, or whatever color — it doesn't matter. It's what's in your heart and head that counts. That's all!"

"Yeaaah," Roxanne said slowly, agreeing with the part about color not making a difference. But she wasn't convinced that the jean jacket wouldn't have made her automatically cool at school.

She could hear in the background now, someone trying to get her mother's attention at work. So it was time for her to stop being a big baby and get off the phone. "I'd better go," Roxanne said.

"You okay?" her mother asked before hanging up.

"Yeah, I'm okay," she answered. Seeing from her watch that she had about fifteen more minutes to kill, Roxanne decided to go to the rest room to wait out the time there.

On her way she passed Rolland, who was so busy talking to the new girl that he didn't even see her. And she wasn't about to call out and try to get his attention!

Seeing that nearly everyone from eighth grade and up was wearing jeans, Roxanne wished now that she had hers on. Jeans and that hot jacket! Surely someone would have noticed her by now if she was wearing that.

Yeah, she mused. I can pick out all the seventh-grade babies. They probably the only ones all decked out in everything new!

A couple of cool-looking girls passed and smiled at her. As one girl whispered something to the other one, and they kept smiling pleasantly, Roxanne changed her mind about looking stupid.

She couldn't read the cool girls' lips, but felt sure that they were admiring her outfit! She *knew* she was looking good when yet another girl walked out of the rest room, looked at her, and smiled.

Going inside, Roxanne was beaming with confidence. Then what did she discover but a girl standing there rocking the very same thing she had on!

So that was what all the smiles and whispers were about! she now realized. She felt pretty stupid, thinking her gear looked so fly to everybody.

As she stood in one corner of the rest room, her twin stood in another with friends. The group looked to Roxanne to be eighth- or ninth-graders. Roxanne was feeling pretty good about wearing the same thing as somebody cool. Of course she had no idea how the *girl* felt about it.

It didn't take long for her to find out. Once the girl spotted her, she gave her a look so cold it sent Roxanne into hiding again!

Only a few minutes out of one booth, Roxanne was now in another! Like a prisoner, she stood locked behind the toilet door, until she heard the girl and her cool friends leaving.

When she finally came out, Roxanne checked her schedule to see where she was supposed to head next. The directions were very confusing. Mrs. Weisbaum had told them that they'd have no problems finding their classes. But it hadn't turned out that way for her.

She was sorry now that she'd wasted so much time. For she had less than five minutes to figure out where she was supposed to be and get there. She thought now how she could have been checking all this out while she was feeling sorry for herself on the phone with her mother, and hiding out in the rest room!

Running down the hall, then up the staircase, she made it to the right floor. But that was about all. She'd no sooner sat down in the classroom than kids started staring at her strangely. Roxanne raised her hand to ask if this was Math 701. It wasn't! A couple of people chuckled as she grabbed her books and went scurrying out of the room.

They laughed when she reached the right room, too. And the teacher gave her what Roxanne thought was a mean look. She didn't follow it up with words however.

Roxanne thought, Shoot, lady, you should be glad I got here at all with those crazy directions! Just then, two more people came flying in, looking confused. See, she thought, with satisfaction. I knew I couldn't be the only one to find those directions wack!

She hoped that nothing too important was said in math today, or in any other class she had coming up. For nothing would stick. All Roxanne could concentrate on now was her disappointment. Six years of longing to be here. And here she sat, wishing she was back at her old school, where she knew her way around.

CHAPTER 6

When they returned to afternoon homeroom, Margarita introduced Roxanne to the other two girls Margarita had met in the morning. Their names were Shanika and Laquita. The kind of names Maxine once joked to Roxanne that nobody could spell but the persons and their mothers!

"Everywhere you turn around the projects, somebody's calling out Shaquilla, Jamika, or something way-out," Maxine had complained, as some young mothers called to their children in the playground. "Nobody around here can be plain Jane anymore!" Maxine had ended, making her laugh.

Shanika, Laquita, and Margarita had looked like a hot group to Roxanne from where they'd sat that morning. But up close they seemed quite ordinary. Laquita was talking a mile a minute, as everybody else struggled to get a word in. Roxanne tagged her "Motormouth," the name Roxanne's father called *her* as a little girl, for talking too much.

Mrs. Weisbaum was telling them now about different activities they could take part in at school.

And to hear Laquita, she was going to be in all of them.

"Yeah," she told them, "I was on the track team at my elementary school and I had the fastest record in the district! Everybody in my family's fast. My sister Latrice and J.J.," she said, rolling off the names of family members.

Whenever anybody else managed to jump in and say something, Laquita found a way to cut them off.

"I'm sorry they don't have a band," Roxanne commented. She had thought there would be one. She wanted to learn to play the flute, an instrument her father played.

"My sister who used to go here, said too many people need braces around our age!" Laquita said, flashing her own set. "You can't play anything good with braces. So they couldn't keep enough kids to make up a band. Plus my sister say, real cool people never wanted to be in no baaand!" she strung out the word, making a face at Roxanne.

"Well, my father happened to play in the band when *he* was in high school!" Roxanne snapped back.

"I want to be in the band in high school!" said Margarita. "I want to be a majorette! Maybe the lead . . ."

" 'Scuse me," Motormouth cut in. "I have a cousin who's a majorette. She goes to Kennedy. I'm going

45

to be a majorette *and* a cheerleader when I get to high school! I can't wait to get there!"

"What I hope's in high school is more guys!" Shanika spoke up. "Seem like every class I was in today there were twice as many girls as boys."

"Wooord!" said Roxanne, thinking about how little she had to report to Maxine.

Laquita took the conversation back. She still had it when the bell rang, setting them free from school, and her mouth!

"Class!" Mrs. Weisbaum said loudly as they were leaving. "Let's all try taking different seats in homeroom tomorrow. It would be good to get to know someone different besides the person you sat next to today."

Roxanne smiled to herself, knowing the lady was just wasting her breath. Everyone would be returning to the same spots tomorrow as surely as if their names were on the chairs. At least I have someone to sit with, she thought. Even though Motormouth's enough to tempt me to go back to the other side of the room tomorrow and just doodle!

Her new friends all went home a different way than Roxanne. So she walked to her bus alone. She passed the black girl and the white girl who had sat in the back. Kenya and Patricia, she'd heard the teacher call them. Their names were all she knew about them so far. But she was determined to find out more.

Roxanne was a little surprised that she didn't see Rolland leaving school. Not that I particularly want to ride home with him or anything like that, she told herself, walking on.

Coming closer to the bus stop, she saw the Door-knockers from that morning! Now she wished Rolland was there! "Just look ahead, look ahead," she chanted. The girls pointed and laughed as they came toward her.

They'd better not touch me! she thought, getting scared. Just why these perfectly strange girls were acting as if they didn't like her, she didn't know.

"I bet it's fake," she heard one say. "That's not her hair!"

She must be crazy! Roxanne said to herself. Calling my hair fake.

"I'll go pull it and see!" one dared to say.

Roxanne froze in her tracks. What's wrong with them? she questioned. *Jealousy*, it came to her. And over *hair*! It had happened before. Girls acting funny with her over stupid hair! It was usually somebody she knew though, telling her that she thought she was cute because she had long hair.

As the girls got closer, Roxanne snapped her finger and made a motion to suggest she'd forgotten something back at school. Then as she was about to turn, someone called out to her. It was Rolland!

"Roxanne!" he said, making her happier than she had ever been to see his face.

Pointing to the girls, who turned now and were walking in another direction, Roxanne told him that she thought they were about to start up with her again.

"For what?" he asked.

"Nothing, I guess," she answered. How could a girl tell a boy that other girls were jealous over something like hair? To Roxanne, this would have made it seem like she thought there was something special about it, too. And she honestly didn't. Short hair, long hair — a girl could be pretty either way, she thought. The girl Rolland had met this morning had a short afro, and she was definitely pretty! Long or short hair can be nice. If girls would only understand . . . she was saying to herself, when Rolland spoke up.

"They're probably jealous of you," he said, as though he could read her mind.

"What made you say that?" she asked, as they walked on.

" 'Cause that's just how people be showin'," he said flatly. "If they start up for no reason, it's usually out of jealousy over your gear or your looks."

"They don't have anything to be jealous of me about," Roxanne insisted.

"They obviously don't see it that way," he said. "I hope you weren't gonna stand 'round and wait for them to rush you."

"No! I was getting ready to go back to the building when you came up," she explained.

"Cool. You heard 'bout the group who jumped a girl on the subway in Brooklyn last week, didn't you?"

"Wasn't that terrible!" Roxanne cried. "*Killing* someone for a pair of earrings!"

"It's crazy!" Rolland agreed. "You used not to hear about stuff like this going down with girls! But now? So watch your back. One-on-one is one thing," he told her. "But when you're outnumbered, the best thing to do is look for safety."

"Hmph!" Roxanne uttered. "I'm not especially interested in any one-on-one either! But if they touch me, I'm not just standing there," she ended boldly.

"Well, I'm here to protect you now," Rolland said, reaching over and touching her shoulder.

"Git outta here!" Roxanne shouted, hitting at him. "You sure wouldn't have been able to protect me in the lunchroom," she said, without thinking. For the last thing she wanted was for Rolland to have some notion that she cared!

"What are you talking about?" he asked.

"Ah, ah!" She struggled now. "Nothing. I just saw you and a new friend."

"Oh, Jewel," he said, casually.

"Jewel?" she repeated. "Hurry! The bus is coming!"

All the seats were taken by the time they got on. Roxanne and Rolland hung on a pole in the center of the bus.

"So what about Miss Jewel?" Roxanne asked smartly.

"She just moved up here from Florida," he told her.

"There's a boy in my class from the South," Roxanne said, for lack of anything better to contribute. "Does Jewel sound funny when she talk?"

"Nothing funny about her to me," he said, getting all dreamy-eyed and making her nauseous! He was acting like he hadn't called himself liking *her* up until this morning!

CHAPTER 7

Maxine was standing in front of the projects when Roxanne and Rolland got off the bus. Roxanne waved Rolland off, so that she and Maxine could talk. She hated having to stand in front of the building to hold a conversation, but couldn't have anyone in the apartment when her mother wasn't home. She didn't have permission to go to anybody else's house whose mother wasn't there, either! It was a wonder, she sometimes thought, that she had even one good friend, with all the rules and regulations she had to live by.

"Why don't you come on home with me, where we can really talk?" Maxine asked, like something had changed in Roxanne's life.

"Now you know I can't go," said Roxanne.

"Even in junior high?" Maxine questioned. "Daaag, didn't your mother hear of the Emancipation Proclamation? When is she going to set you free?"

"Don't be talking about my mother, Maxine," Roxanne said, defensively.

"I just don't understand what's so terrible about your best friend being at your house when your mother's not there. Or you being at theirs!"

"My mother says anything can happen," said Roxanne.

"Anything can happen out here, too," Maxine responded.

Roxanne paused, not really knowing what to say to that. Maybe Mommie won't either, she considered, storing the thought away to put to her mother later.

"So how is Riverdale Junior High?" Maxine continued.

"Oh, cool!" Roxanne answered, trying to sound like she'd made a big hit there today. "How's your school?"

"Cool, too!" said Maxine. "And oh! Guess what?"

"What?"

"I met this real cute guy who sings lead in the Harlem Boys' Choir!"

"Guess who met a new girl?" Roxanne moved the conversation along, hoping Maxine wouldn't want to know who *she'd* met special.

"Who?" Maxine asked.

"Mr. Rolland!" she answered. "Her name's Jewel."

"That's a nice name," Maxine commented.

"Just a name to me," Roxanne responded, shrugging.

"Well what did Rolland say?" Maxine asked. "He say he like her or what?"

"I don't know and I don't care!" Roxanne snapped, starting to wish she'd never mentioned Rolland and the girl.

"You're not getting jealous now?" Maxine asked next, really starting to make Roxanne mad.

"Why would I be jealous of Rolland?" she asked, laughing at the suggestion.

"You sound like you're angry at *something*," Maxine continued. "You're always saying how you wish Rolland would stop buggin' you. So why you sounding angry since he's talking to another girl?"

"I refuse to even talk about this anymore!" Roxanne told her.

"I know how it is," Maxine ended. "Sometimes you feel like you don't like a person. Then when somebody else start liking him, you wonder. You know?"

"No, I don't know!" Roxanne shouted.

Maxine really was her number-one homegirl. But still, she made her mad sometimes. Roxanne felt that the star program that Maxine had been in at P.S. 9 gave her a big head. While Roxanne was willing to admit that Maxine was much smarter than her bookwise, she felt that they were even when it came to knowing the facts of life! Maxine seldom acted like it though.

"So what else is new?" she asked Roxanne now, sounding as if she knew she was getting on Roxanne's nerves.

"If we can change the subject, one important thing that happened today is that three girls tried to jump me!" Roxanne said, building up the story a little.

"Three?" Maxine exclaimed.

"Yeah. This morning and this afternoon, they were bothering me. And I hadn't done *one* thing to them! If they start up again, I don't know *what* I should do!"

"Call their bluff," suggested Maxine, as if it were no big deal.

"You heard me say there were *three*!" Roxanne said with annoyance.

"Which is all the more reason to go for it," Maxine said. "They probably just bluffing! Stand in one face at a time, and see what happens! Scary people always travel in a pack like that. But the minute there's only one, they're ready to back off!"

"I don't know, Maxine," Roxanne said slowly.

"Trust me!" she snapped. "You have to let people know that you're not scared of them. Even sometimes when you are. Now what else happened today? Any guys say anything to you?"

"Yeah," Roxanne answered, hoping she would let it rest there. But of course, she didn't.

"Who?" Maxine wanted to know.

"Oh, just a couple of guys," Roxanne said, thinking to herself that it wasn't altogether untrue. A couple of boys *had* said something to her today. The one who snapped on her eyebrows, and the one with the stupid "light skin" line. Just please don't let her ask me *what* boys, or what they said, she thought.

Boobie came up just in time. Maxine may have met a cute new guy at school, but she was still smiling mighty hard over ole Boobie, Roxanne thought.

"What's up?" he asked.

"I'd better go," Roxanne told Maxine after saying hello to Boobie. "Check you later."

"I'll probably drop off the book I finished!" Maxine said.

"Just make sure it's before my mother comes home!" Roxanne advised. "Or hide it when you come in," she ended, laughing.

When Roxanne reached her floor, she eased out of the elevator quietly. She was trying to keep Mrs. Edwards, her next door neighbor, from hearing her come in. Roxanne worried that Mrs. Edwards would have something for her to do. An elderly widow who lived alone, Mrs. Edwards didn't get out much. She had once been robbed in the elevator, so she was nervous about going anywhere alone. Roxanne went to the store for her, the post office, and ran other errands.

She often wished that some other young person lived on the seventh floor besides her. Because Mrs. Edwards had just about worn her legs out! But then she realized that *someone* had to help the poor widow.

"Roooxanne," she heard her call now, just as she turned her key in the lock.

"Yes, Mrs. Edwards?" she replied, turning around slowly and smiling over how hard it was to get by her.

"I was wondering if your mother had a stick of margarine I could borrow?"

"I'm pretty sure she does," Roxanne said politely. "I'll be right back."

She was relieved that this was all Mrs. Edwards wanted, and that she didn't have to go trotting right back downstairs. Only one elevator had been working when she came up. So she'd had to wait a long time. When the one working elevator finally came, it smelled real bad. This was something else Roxanne hated about living here — the elevator situation. Not only were they dangerous, but kids sometimes used them for a rest room. So you often had to watch your back as well as hold your nose.

The phone was ringing when she returned from taking Mrs. Edwards the margarine. It was her father.

"How's my big junior high girl?" he asked. "I've been waiting by the phone, hoping you'd call me and tell me!"

"Oh, I was going to!" she said. "I had to run next door to Mrs. Edwards first. She needed some margarine."

"It's sweet of you to help Mrs. Edwards," her father said — something he'd repeated often. Her father had been furious the day the old lady had been robbed. He had taken off downstairs, hoping to catch the thief himself. "The lowest of the lowest," was what he'd called whoever it was that robbed Mrs. Edwards.

This had all happened the year before when her father still lived at home. He lived in Yonkers now, not far from the projects. With him being so close, things went pretty smoothly for Roxanne. She saw him every week, and talked to him almost every day.

After telling her father all about her new school, she mentioned that she wanted him to drive her and Rolland to the mall in Westchester one afternoon. "So that I can prove to the boy that there are malls up here like there are down South!" she explained.

"So Rolland's going to be your number-one friend in junior high, too, huh?" he teased.

"Daddy, git outta here!" she shouted. "I told you before that I don't like no Rolland! I just want you to take us to the mall. And another thing, the boy met a new girl today. And he's not thinking about me!"

"Bet she's not pretty as you!" Her father kept it up. "Rolland's got to see that!"

Roxanne brought up the Doorknockers, the first thing she could think of to get him on another subject. But this turned out to be a mistake.

"You want me to start picking you up after school?" he asked, right away.

Oh, Lordy, she thought. I said the wrong thing now! Scared as boys my age are of girls' fathers, I'd never meet anybody new with my daddy picking me up every day!

"You know I'm home early enough to do it," he said.

"Rolland looks out for me!" Roxanne came up with quickly.

"My man Rolland," this made him say.

"Oh, Daddy, stop," she said, laughing.

"Well, you just let me know," her father said firmly. "If those girls or anybody else bothers you, you know I'll be out there in a flash!"

* * *

When her mother came in, Roxanne repeated all she'd told her father about school. All but the Doorknocker story. She didn't want to chance her mother offering to come to school for her, too!

Going over everything twice was about the hardest part to her of having a mother in one place and a father in another. This and dividing up holiday time. Sometimes she couldn't make up her mind which parent she wanted to be with on a holiday. So they would have to make it up for her.

When her father first moved, Roxanne felt guilty. For there had been times that she'd secretly wished him away. During the summer when everybody in the projects played late in the park, she always had to come inside early. Maxine and other girls who didn't have fathers living at home were free. They could stay outside way past dark! But soon as the sun went down, her father would be leaning out the window, calling for her to come upstairs. And when it seemed like she wasn't moving fast enough, he'd come down after her!

So Roxanne started wishing she lived with just her mother. Then when this came true, it was another story. She felt bad for having wished such a thing. Anyhow, it turned out that she was mighty wrong in thinking she was going to have more rope with her mother. Because her mother stayed on her case the same as if her father were around!

Now that school had started, Roxanne wouldn't bother trying to get outside during the week at all. By the time she did her homework and flipped between *Oprah* and *Donahue*, it would be getting dark outside — the time she had to be upstairs!

CHAPTER 8

Little changed for Roxanne the first few weeks at Riverdale Junior High. One thing that she was feeling pretty good over was calling the Doorknockers' bluff as Maxine suggested.

The girls had kept up their silliness for days, giggling and making faces whenever they saw her. But they would never say anything directly to her. Roxanne was growing anxious to have it out with them, but it seemed she never would. "They just want to keep picking at me from a distance!" she kept repeating to Maxine.

Finally, one day when Roxanne was leaving school, she faced off with them. Traveling alone (pretty much how it had been since Rolland met Jewel) the Doorknockers came walking up behind her.

"It's too hot for those cowboy boots," one said.

"Maybe she's in the rodeo," another one joked about the boots Roxanne wore.

Roxanne stopped and waited for them. They

seemed surprised. Spinning around at the point that they reached her, she faced the one closest to her.

"Excuse me!" Roxanne said boldly. "You got a problem with me? Or you?" she said turning to another girl. "Or you, or you?" she asked, staring them down one by one. This was one time that she was pleased to be tall, for she was able to look down at each of them. The girls were either scared or so stunned that they didn't know what to do! They got out of her face immediately. And they walked away quietly, looking embarrassed.

Since then, they had been walking by Roxanne acting normal. And along with that, one of them had bought the same jean jacket Roxanne now owned.

"After managing to beg my father for the jacket," she told Maxine, "a Doorknocker goes and bites it! The thing doesn't even seem special to me now!"

"Every time you see their little group, you must get tickled," Maxine had said. And Roxanne truly did!

She'd had the pleasure one morning, of them seeing her on the bus talking to Sharon Tyson, a fly girl from the projects. Sharon was known as a super cool person at school. She stood out. No one else at Riverdale Junior High had her hair twisted in locks but Sharon! Roxanne would have liked to look so bold. But she could just *hear* her mother's mouth, if she tried wearing that hairstyle.

When the Doorknockers had checked her out, sitting beside Sharon, they had stared for the longest time. They were wondering, Roxanne was sure, how it was that a ninth-grader could be giving her the time of day!

Sharon had taken the seat beside her when they first got on the bus. But not without Roxanne looking up like a little puppy with pleading eyes, and patting for her to please sit beside her. Sharon had turned, checking out the scene around her, before finally sitting down.

Roxanne found it embarrassing to sweat Sharon like she'd done. But she felt it was well worth it after the Doorknockers spotted them. It was good, she figured, for them to see that she knew somebody important like Sharon!

Sharon had told her that her father had their family on a waiting list for an apartment in Riverdale. But Roxanne didn't believe her. Nearly everybody from the projects (including her mother) was always talking about moving.

"As soon as I can save up, I'm getting out of here!" Roxanne's mother had said over and over. Some days she screamed it. She'd scream it when kids jammed up the elevators; scream it every time she heard that someone else had been robbed in the building; scream it when there was garbage left on the floor around the incinerator; scream it when the people upstairs played loud music all night.

These times, and many more, Roxanne had heard her mother declare that she was getting out of Bailey Hills Projects! And her mother wasn't the only one dying to go.

So Roxanne figured Sharon was just one more person wishing, something riding the bus to Riverdale certainly could make you do!

Sharon had promised that she was going to show her around school. That, too, Roxanne soon realized, was just more empty lipping. The girl hadn't said a word to her since! Not that she truly expected her to. As a rule, ninth-graders ignored seventh-graders around school. But Roxanne didn't care. She was surviving.

One thing that she liked a lot about junior high was changing classes (now that she knew where she was going!). It was cool, not having to look in the same teacher's face all day. And she suspected the feeling was vice versa.

It didn't take long to pick her favorite teacher. It was Mr. Hill, her history teacher. She liked him because he knew how to let up and not be so serious all the time. Mr. Hill told a pretty good joke, too. Nothing side-breaking, but good enough to make the class more relaxed.

He had started the year off telling the class that

many of their lessons wouldn't be coming from the textbook. Mr. Hill had Roxanne reading a lot more than what she and Maxine called the sweep-aways (romance novels, that swept them away!). Maxine's sister ordered the books from a romance club, and they all had read them secretly.

Now Roxanne was reading a whole lot more. Mr. Hill had her reading the newspaper daily, and she was also watching the evening news. She had learned that she couldn't slack off, either. Not if she wanted to sound cool when the discussions started up in Mr. Hill's class. Roxanne couldn't see having people talk all around her and not being able to participate. But she was learning that there were kids who didn't mind.

"Not me though!" she'd told Maxine. "I want to be in on what's going on, and not sitting there like a dummy with nothing to say. So I keep up on what's happening!"

"I've been doing that all along," Maxine told her. "I read the papers, every magazine I can find, *everything*! Even when I'm watching television, I like to have something to read."

Roxanne had never thought of this before. But now she, too, had started reading and watching television at the same time. As Maxine had pointed out, so much of what you watched on TV was just like something you'd seen before. A good book on the side kept you from being bored.

Roxanne finally had to break down and tell her father to forget about the trip to the mall. He kept asking her when she wanted to go, and she hardly ever saw Rolland anymore! She had ridden home from school with him maybe two times since he started talking to Jewel. But that was about it. One morning she ran into the two of them on the way to school. Since then, she had been leaving earlier, like today.

Leaving early had turned out to be a plus. The bus wasn't as crowded for one thing. And instead of riding with the regular rowdy crew, she rode with older women on their way to work in Riverdale. The women were all black, and most of them West Indian — like a girl in her English class whom she loved to hear speak. There was a special rhythm in her voice.

Roxanne liked listening to the women talk, too. And it wasn't just how they sounded, but the stories they told.

She would have her mother cracking up at night about the way the ladies got down on the people they worked for. "If some of those people heard how they trashed them," she'd told her mother, "they might not have a job anymore!"

"But then they might," her mother suggested. "Because from what you tell me you hear them saying, the people in Riverdale would be pretty lost without them!"

Roxanne had told Maxine about the ladies, too. And the two of them had dreamed of what it must have been like for children who had a maid. "Oh, I can just see it!" Maxine said. "Coming home from school every day to find your room all cleaned up."

"And someone waiting with milk and cookies," Roxanne added. And they had laughed and dreamed on.

The ladies always gave Roxanne warm grandmotherly smiles when they saw her in the morning. She had taken a seat as close as she could today, not wanting to miss a thing!

"Yeees," one woman was saying to another. "I tell that chile of mine, jus' keep foolin' 'roun' and not studyin' and you'll end up goin' nowhere! And it'll be poke and grits at every meal! Pokin' out ya mouth and grittin' ya teeth!" she ended, laughing.

"How 'bout some air puddin' for dessert?" the other lady threw in.

Roxanne was laughing as heartily as if they were talking directly to her.

Pulling herself together, she looked to the back to see what else was going on. She was surprised to spot someone from homeroom. It was Kenya, the black half of the integrated two from the back of the room! She was sitting with a woman who Roxanne decided was Kenya's mother.

Kenya took gym with Roxanne, but Roxanne still hadn't gotten to know her. Throughout the whole gym period, Kenya stayed near the teacher, exercising alone. She had done this since the day she'd had a run-in with a girl named Tara.

Tara had snapped on Kenya's sneakers, calling them skips. When Kenya threw her to the floor, it took the teacher and two or three more people to get her off Tara. Since then, Kenya pretty much stayed in her corner. One day Roxanne had started in her direction, but Kenya turned her back to her. Roxanne didn't press it, knowing in her heart that what she'd really wanted was to get into the girl's business.

She was trying hard to catch her eye now, but Kenya kept looking away. It was as though she had seen her and simply didn't want to speak to her.

It came to Roxanne, that Kenya might have felt funny over her mother going to Riverdale to do housework. You hardly even saw black maids on *TV* anymore. Not unless the story went way back in time. Just the same, everybody knew there were still black maids. For sure, everyone riding the bus to school in Riverdale did. A whole lot of women cleaned other people's houses up the hill. But shoot! Roxanne thought. There was no reason to be embarrassed about it. Hard as times were, a job was a job. And she'd be the first to tell Kenya that.

The job Roxanne's own mother had was her first one in an office. Before this job, she had baby-sat for different people in the projects. And talk about misery? Roxanne used to get so tired of little whining kids being at her house. But as she got older, she could appreciate her mother doing what she could at the time. For if her mother hadn't worked, it might not have been possible for Roxanne to have the things her mother had given her over the years.

She was going to find a way to let Kenya know that her mother and all those ladies seemed pretty special. *If* she got to know her better!

When they reached the school bus stop, Roxanne decided that she was going to walk up to Kenya and say something! Not just to be nosey, she told herself, but to start a friendship. For it was time she added to her list of friends, more than the three pitiful names there so far: Margarita, and (once in a while) Laquita and Shanika!

"Hi, Kenya," Roxanne said, trying to sound cheerful. "I see you in homeroom and in gym. But this is the first time I've seen you on the bus. Was that your mother?"

"No. That was my grandmother," Kenya answered, sounding like she didn't want to be bothered.

"Ohhh," Roxanne said, refusing to give up. "How far do you two travel?"

"Not far," came her short answer.

"I'm Roxanne."

"I know," she said. "The same way you know I'm Kenya," she added. "Mrs. Weisbaum *does* call it out each and every morning!"

"True," Roxanne acknowledged lightheartedly. "I love your name," she told Kenya.

"It's African," she stated proudly. "All my sisters and brothers have African names."

"How many do you have?" Roxanne asked.

"Two sisters — two brothers. And you?"

"I'm the only one in my family," Roxanne told her.

"I'm the only one living in the Bronx with my grandmother. The rest are in Manhattan," Kenya explained, a sad expression coming across her face. She was quiet for a moment. Then she asked, "How do you like this school?"

"Seems pretty neat so far," Roxanne said.

"Yeah, it's neat all right," Kenya agreed. "And I mean in every way. I've never been to a school as clean as this one. Or a neighborhood!"

"Yeah. It's pretty nice around here all right," Roxanne said, looking toward a fancy building. A door-man was carrying the books of a teenage girl as she walked to a van. "Hmph! Hmph! Hmph!" Roxanne uttered, smiling and shaking her head over it.

"Ain't that nothing?" Kenya commented. "Some people can't carry their own things two steps."

"Wooord," went Roxanne. "They're a lot of rich people in Riverdale, you know."

"You live around here?" Kenya asked, as though she thought Roxanne was including herself in the rich group.

"Girl, I don't mean *me*!" Roxanne hurried and said. "Didn't you see where I got on?"

"No," Kenya answered.

"I'm from Bailey Hills," she explained. "A lot o' people who go to our school are from the projects. But most are from Riverdale. Compared to those of us from the projects, they may be rich. I guess."

"I saw this one boy being dropped off by a maid!" exclaimed Kenya.

"You lie!" cried Roxanne.

"If I'm lying I'm flying!" she declared. "And as he was walking toward the school building, his maid came rushing after him, telling him he'd forgotten his naive water!"

"Forgot his what?" asked Roxanne.

"Store-bought water spelled backward!" Kenya explained. "EVIAN!"

"Oh, that's funny!" Roxanne laughed as they walked on.

"The boy leaned over, hugged the lady, and went, 'Oh, thank you, Nanna! I don't know what I'd do without you!' "

"Oh, stop it!" Roxanne shouted, wiping away tears from her eyes.

"Lil' spoiled rascal," Kenya continued as they walked into the building. "The people my grandmother work for have three children. They go to a private school downtown somewhere. They get chauffeured all the way into Manhattan in a *real* limousine — not no regular car like Nanna's boy stepped out of! I'm talkin' a stretch! They what you call high rich. Somebody being drove around in a regular car, low rich. You know?"

"I think I know," Roxanne said, smiling as Kenya grew on her more and more. The girl had such a way of putting things!

"My grandmother says that even though the children she works for go to school dressed like they're going to business — in suits, ties, the whole works — it doesn't make them one bit better than me! 'Cause goodness comes from the inside not the outside."

Roxanne listened, wondering where she had heard something similar. It was from her mother, she remembered, looking down at her jean jacket.

The jacket never changed a thing in her world, just as her mother said it wouldn't. It was only some dumb material sewed together and decorated with junk. She was about ready to give it a rest!

When they reached homeroom, Kenya signaled that she was going to the back of the room to join her friend Pat.

"Later!" Roxanne said, heading for her usual spot, too.

She was more anxious than ever now to find out more about Kenya and Pat, and how they got to be so close.

Roxanne waved good-bye to the both of them when it was time to leave for first period. Hopefully Kenya would see in her smile, a sign that she wanted to get to know her better.

CHAPTER 9

Roxanne didn't see Kenya again until gym period. When she told her that she'd looked for her at lunchtime, Kenya explained that she'd gone up to where her grandmother worked for the first time. Kenya had Roxanne cracking up, as she told about the hard-way-to-go she had getting into the fancy building. She and Roxanne were standing at the side of the gym in Kenya's familiar spot, as she told her story:

"At first the doorman wanted to know if I was a messenger!" she said, laughing. "I answered, NO! 'A baby-sitter?' he asked. Then, 'Are you doing something for someone here?' he goes! I was about ready to say, 'Mister, if you don't get out my face and let me buzz up to my grandmother, I *am* going to be doing something for somebody here. And I'm looking right at him!' " she said, making Roxanne laugh so hard it hurt.

"Now I could understand if there was something about me that looked dangerous," Kenya continued. "But look at me!" she shouted, spreading her arms.

"Who I look like I could hurt? There was no reason in the world for that man to put me through all that! I told my grandmother just meet me downstairs the next time. 'Cause if that ever happens again, I might say something to somebody grown that I have no business!"

"I know how you feel!" said Roxanne. "What kills me is to have somebody look at me funny when I walk into a store! I've never stolen anything in my whole life! So it hurts to have someone treating me like they think I might!"

"Wooord," said Kenya. "But in spite of being dissed by the doorman, I had a nice time with my grandmother. She let me have a tour of the premises and it's a mansion! After lunch, the two of us sipped tea," she said, motioning with her hand and trying to sound proper. "We were like any two rich ladies on a *lazy* afternoon," she added, laughing.

"My grandmother brought out the good china and everything! She said it's important that I know about such things as sitting properly and using the right piece of silverware. I said, 'Grandma, just when am I *ever* going to be called on to use stuff like this?' And she goes, 'You never know, baby. You never know. The secret is to be ready when opportunity come knocking. Opportunity come knocking, you don't wanna be sittin' wondering whether to pick up the fork or the spoon!' "

"Your grandmother sounds like she's a real trip," Roxanne said, smiling warmly.

"She's special all right," Kenya agreed.

"Yeah. All those ladies on the bus going to work seem special," Roxanne added. "I wish I had a grandmother who lived here. One's dead. And the other one's in Georgia."

"Yeah," said Kenya. "Ain't nothing better than having a sweet grandmama to turn to," she ended with a sigh.

By now, another girl in gym class was watching them, like she wanted to come join them. The girl had only started at Riverdale Junior High that week, and seemed nervous over her newness. So Roxanne smiled and motioned for her to come on over. She probably thinks I'm somebody cool, since I'm the one who called her over, Roxanne thought. But she'll soon be finding out that with her no-name sneakers and all, Kenya's the cool one standing here!

"You all know how to jump double dutch?" the girl asked when she reached them.

"Can a fly fly?" Kenya cracked.

"Yeah. We'd better do something constructive," Roxanne said, taking hold of the ropes. "Or the gym teacher's going to come over here and make us take laps for standing around running our mouths."

"Exercising your lips!" the girl joked, making them laugh.

"What's your name?" Roxanne asked her as she walked toward the center of the ropes.

"I tell everybody to call me N.E.," she whispered. "Please don't ask what it stands for."

"You're with good people!" Roxanne said, holding onto the ropes like she wasn't moving until she told them.

"It's Necessary!" the girl said, even softer.

"Necessary to tell?" asked Roxanne.

"That's the girl's name, dummy!" snapped Kenya. "Where you been?"

Roxanne sucked in her cheeks to keep from laughing.

"Don't feel bad!" Kenya spoke up. "I had a boy in my class one time named Tree! Lots of people have parents who named them something strange. I'm glad mine stopped at the homeland! Just don't worry about it N.E. You can change it when you grown. That's what Tree says he's doing."

By now Margarita had walked up. She wanted to jump rope, too. But Roxanne told her she'd have to wait her turn. N.E. was first. As the girl started jumping, Roxanne thought, DAAAG! People be having all kind of burdens. Having to worry about their sneakers. Their names. All kinds of things!

Her name was strange, but Necessary sure could burn, Roxanne decided. She and Kenya were cutting the ropes so fast they whistled. And N.E. wasn't missing a beat. Faster and faster, they turned. And N.E. kept right up with them, snapping her feet from side to side and bouncing into the air as they sang:

Go on
Go on
Go N.E.
Go N.E.
You bad
You bad
Fly girl's here
Fly girl's there
Fly girl's jumpin'
all in the air
HARRIET
MALCOLM
MARTIN LUTHER KING
Raise their names
and do your thing!
On one foot
jump 'round and 'round
then stoop down and
touch the ground!
Go N.E.

Go N.E.
You bad
You bad . . .

Soon they had the whole crowd around them, including certified cool people *and* the teacher! Roxanne knew a lot of girls from the projects who could double dutch, but she'd never seen anybody work the ropes like N.E. Homegirl was cooking!

"Girl, you look like you've been practicing for days," Margarita said when N.E. stopped.

"Nothing else to do around where I live," N.E. explained. "The park's all busted up — there's no center to go to. So boys play basketball, *if* they can find a hoop intact! And girls, we jump rope."

"That's how it goes everywhere," Kenya threw in. "You have to learn to use what you got."

"Wisdom! I'm naming you," Roxanne said behind that.

"No! Save that for my middle name!" N.E. joked. "It go so good with Necessary!"

This is it! Roxanne decided, standing and laughing with these three girls. This was going to be her group from now on — the main people she was sticking with every day!

It was amazing how smoothly they had pulled off the double-dutch numbers without practice. Maybe that's how friendship has to come, she thought. Just naturally.

The gym teacher was so impressed with their jumping, that she asked if they would be willing to teach others in the class.

Kenya wanted to know if the principal would be paying them.

The teacher laughed, appearing glad to see Kenya come alive in gym again. And Roxanne was happy about it all, too. Eighth-grade girls took gym this period also. So it meant that some seventh-graders had something to show off for a change!

Roxanne was surprised though that the teacher had asked them to give demonstrations. Back at P.S. 9, a teacher once made her and some girls from the projects stop double dutching. It happened after other girls (who didn't know how) got jealous and started complaining.

"No fancy jumping in the school yard," the teacher had announced shaking her finger in their faces. Roxanne remembered being hurt by the teacher's action. It was only in telling the story at home, that Roxanne learned that she and the projects girls hadn't done anything wrong.

"It's a gift," her father had explained, when she tearfully told what had happened at school. "The way you and your friends can jump rope is a special talent you've been given."

"Like you have at playing the flute?" Roxanne had looked up at him and asked.

"Yes," he answered. "And nobody can take a special gift away."

"Nobody?" she pressed.

"Not even the teacher," he said. "If she has a problem with your fancy jumping at school, save it until you get back home. Then you and your friends can double dutch to your heart's content. Nobody can take a special talent away," he repeated, giving her a hug. "The only way you can lose it, is if you don't use it."

CHAPTER 10

Roxanne, Kenya, Margarita, and N.E. were sticking together. They were all in the cafeteria now, except Kenya, who was absent today.

They weren't a closed group. Most of the time, Kenya's friend Patricia stuck with them, too. There were days though, that Kenya and Pat simply went off together alone. This bothered Margarita and N.E., but it didn't faze Roxanne. Her feeling was that Kenya and Pat were tight before Kenya started sticking with them. And Kenya obviously didn't believe in dropping an old friend for a new one, like Roxanne felt Rolland had done to her in a way.

All his talk in the beginning of school about looking out for her, and now he was nowhere to be seen! Roxanne had this much to say for Rolland though, he wasn't hung up on stupid hair! Jewel had cut her afro even shorter now. With her smooth dark skin and short 'fro, she looked to Roxanne as royal as her name sounded. So at least Rolland saw that light skin or dark, long hair or short, one look was as pretty as the other. Roxanne had to respect him for this. But still, he didn't have to go and drop her. This, she didn't think was right.

'Course she did have to admit that she and Margarita didn't have too much to say to Laquita and Shanika anymore in homeroom. But then, she had never really gotten too close with the two. Margarita had though.

The problem with Pat was that she never seemed completely comfortable in the group when Kenya wasn't around. And for some reason, Kenya was always absent! Sometimes when she returned she would tell them she'd been sick. Then there were times that she gave no explanation. Margarita, N.E., and Roxanne talked about it, and how it was weird for someone to be absent so much.

Something else that Roxanne found odd was that Kenya didn't have a telephone. Roxanne knew some families in the projects who were pretty bad off. But even *they* had a telephone! So one thing that she had figured out about Kenya was that her family was having a hard time.

When Kenya didn't show up in homeroom this morning, Roxanne guessed that Pat wouldn't be with them for lunch. And sure enough, Pat walked up to their meeting spot at noon with a story. She told them that she had to go to the library to look up some material.

"Aren't you going to eat first?" Roxanne asked her.

"I'm not in the mood for anything," she said. Roxanne went along with it. But she knew that what Pat wasn't in the mood for was trying to hang without Kenya. Margarita and N.E. always pressed her for information about Kenya when Kenya wasn't there. They had learned better than to ask Kenya too many questions. But with Pat they pressed on. She had told them a dozen times that she didn't know any more than they did. But still they kept digging.

Like Margarita and N.E., Roxanne wondered if Pat didn't know more, too. Because whenever Kenya returned from being absent, the two would be huddled together talking. But since she didn't have the nerve to bug Kenya about it, Roxanne didn't think it was fair to pick Pat for information.

"I still believe she knows more than she lets on!" Margarita said, once the three of them were settled at their table in the cafeteria.

"I knew you were going to start up on that again," said Roxanne.

"Well, it's probably true," N.E. chimed in. "Pat's holding something back from us."

"What I can't figure, is why Mrs. Weisbaum got to be so closemouthed," said Margarita. "*Twice* I've asked her why Kenya was out, and she pretended not to hear me! I hate a closemouthed teacher, who won't tell you about your friends."

You wouldn't feel that way if it was *your* business being spread," Roxanne said, laughing.

"I wouldn't care what all my friends knew about me," said N.E.

"You wouldn't want *everybody* to know *everything*," stated Roxanne.

"Well Miss Patricia is one person who I think *does* know everything about Kenya!" Margarita snapped.

"Maybe not!" Roxanne tried telling them.

"Well, why she never wanna be with us when Kenya's out?" asked N.E.

"The girl obviously just feels more comfortable when Kenya's here," said Roxanne. "That's all. Even then, she's the only white one, remember."

"Black and white can be friends," said Margarita. "Just like us — Dominican and black. Me? I don't pick and choose. Just whosoever's cool."

"I had black, white, all kind of friends when I first started school," N.E. began. "Then . . ."

"You all started going different ways!" Roxanne cut in.

"How you know?" N.E. asked.

" 'Cause it's my story, too," Roxanne explained. "Everybody starts out friends in kindergarten. Then by third or fourth grade, zoom, it all changes!"

"Sometimes one person thinks another person doesn't want to talk with them, when they haven't ever gone up to find out," said Margarita.

"True," Roxanne agreed.

" 'Cause like if I hadn't said something to you the first day of school, we might *still* not be speaking!" Margarita pointed out. "You should have seen her, N.E., sitting looking all stuck-up in homeroom!"

"That's not true!" Roxanne said firmly. "I was sitting looking scared. Then you pulled me in."

"Just as I was looking scared when you pulled *me* in," N.E. reminded Roxanne.

"OOOH! OOOH! OOOH!" Margarita began all of a sudden, giggling and twisting around her seat. "There he goes!" she whispered with excitement.

"Stop carrying on like some loosey-goosey!" Roxanne ordered, as Margarita pointed to a boy, she'd told them she liked. He was in her first-period class and named Malik.

"Oooooh! OOOh!" she continued. "I'm gonna die!"

"Girl, calm down and stop acting so wack!" Roxanne said. Then, just as she had about settled her down, N.E. spotted Thad, a boy *she* liked.

Now Roxanne had the both of them to work on. She really wished Kenya were here today now. Because these two were losing it.

"Come on. Let's go!" Margarita said, ready to jump

up and follow the boys, who were leaving the cafeteria.

"Girl, I'm not through with my food yet!" said Roxanne.

But this didn't matter to Margarita, or to N.E., who were both on their feet already!

Roxanne got up, too, and gathered her tray. Otherwise she was going to be left there alone.

When they caught up with Margarita and N.E.'s dreamboys in the hallway, neither guy as much as blinked in their direction. And heaven knows they should have! Roxanne was thinking. The way these two were *performing*!

Roxanne tried to tell them that laughing and talking loud like they were doing looked silly. But they kept it up.

"Will you all chill?" she finally shouted. Seeing that they weren't about to, she said, "Oh, do what you wanna!" Putting some distance between herself and them, she walked ahead.

They were embarrassing her. All she could do was hope that Kenya hurried back. Because with these two acting this crazy over boys who hadn't even spoken to them, she hated to think what was going to happen if they did!

"You'll be acting the same way when you see somebody *you* like!" Margarita said, after she and

N.E. ran and caught up with Roxanne again. "Just wait and see."

"Yeah!" N.E. joined in. "You'll see. And every time you pass the person at school, you'll get this funny feeling that's some kind of wonderful," she ended, sighing deeply.

CHAPTER 11

Kenya returned after being out a week. As usual, she walked up and gave Mrs. Weisbaum a note. Roxanne and Margarita went to the back, taking two seats beside Kenya and Pat.

Margarita had bragged to Roxanne that she was going to "get some answers out of Kenya this morning!" Roxanne looked over at her now, waiting to see if she was going to go through with it.

Finally Margarita started up. "Just what is going on with you, girlfriend?" she asked, facing Kenya.

Without commenting right away, Kenya simply glared at her.

"Just what is the deal?" Margarita pressed on. "We're all supposed to be friends, aren't we?"

"I told you before that it's my business why I'm out!" Kenya snapped.

"All I did was ask," Margarita said, shrugging her shoulders.

"And I answered," Kenya said flatly, making Roxanne glad that she'd kept her mouth shut.

"Let's go up to Angelo's for pizza at lunchtime!"

Pat said, trying to change the subject quickly.

"No. We have to eat inside!" Margarita stated, then went on to explain why.

"You can count me out!" Kenya announced. "I'm not down for hanging in the lunchroom while you and N.E. play *Love Connection*! It doesn't take prancing around guys for them to notice you!"

"You make it sound so bad!" said Roxanne.

"I'm just telling it like it is," said Kenya. "See, I grew up in Manhattan."

"That doesn't mean a thing!" Margarita fired. "Besides. Nobody cares where you come from. You're in the Bronx now!"

"Listen," Kenya said, smiling. "I'm not trying to be in your business. 'Cause I can't stand for anyone to try to get in mine. So hey! Like Bobby Brown sings, "It's Your Perogative!" You all can flirt around in the cafeteria much as you please. Just don't look for me!"

True to her word, there was no sign of Kenya at lunch period. This of course meant no Pat either. It seemed to Roxanne that their little group was crumbling, slowly but surely.

After a week of following Margarita and N.E. around during lunch period, Roxanne was ready to admit that Kenya was right. What they were doing *was* stupid! Soon the weather would be changing, and there would be no choice but to eat inside. But a few more warm days remained. Days that she didn't want to spend in the cafeteria boy-watching!

After school, Roxanne stood in front of the building, where Margarita and N.E. met before going home. This was as good a time as any, she thought, to tell them how she was feeling about their lunch routine.

"I'm tired of that cafeteria food every day," she began, once Margarita and N.E. got there.

"It's not the food that matters," said Margarita. "You need to git a life, girlfriend!"

"I don't see anything you all are doing that's so special!" Roxanne shot back at her.

"At least we trying to make something happen!" said N.E. "You need to pick out someone to like, too."

Jeepers creepers! Roxanne was thinking, when she turned to see who was calling her. It was Rolland. He was coming their way now.

"Hmmm," went Margarita. "Seem like you may not have to search far!"

"Git outta here!" Roxanne said, laughing. "That's only Rolland.

"OOONLY!" crooned N.E.

"Rolland, this is Margarita and N.E.," Roxanne said when he reached them.

"Long time no see," Rolland began. "I wanted to

warn you about tomorrow — Halloween!" he said facing Roxanne. "According to what I hear, some wild stuff gon' be going on 'round here. A lot of people are staying home — including me!"

"Instead of being scared, I look forward to it," shouted Margarita. "It used to get wild at my elementary school, too!"

"Well, trouble or no trouble," said Roxanne. "I'm one person who'll be here tomorrow. I know better than to think I can stay home just because I want to, because my mother don't play that. To stay in my bed I have to be almost dead!" she joked.

"Well, I won't have any trouble with my moms," Rolland said — something Roxanne knew automatically.

"The boys are the craziest ones on Halloween!" N.E. stated. "They be throwing eggs at one another and all. Even 'round my way they throw them. Good eggs! When they know good and well that their family doesn't have food to play with like that!"

"Woooord," said Margarita.

"Well, anyhow, Roxanne, don't say I didn't warn you," Rolland ended. "Later," he said, starting to walk on.

N.E. began bumping Roxanne, whispering, "Go! Go! Follow the guy, Roxanne!"

"Yeah," Margarita said, joining in. "Why you letting him slip away?"

"That's just Rolland," Roxanne tried to explain. "Someone I've known since forever! And another thing — he likes somebody else in seventh grade!"

"Sooo?" went Margarita. "He was smiling pretty bodaciously at you!"

"And worrying about you having trouble tomorrow," N.E. added.

"I'll see you two crazies tomorrow!" Roxanne said, laughing and shaking her head. "I meant what I said about chillin' on that cafeteria thing though!" she repeated before leaving.

At supper, Roxanne thought she'd just test the "staying home tomorrow," out on her mother. Just for fun!

"You know better than to even ask me any foolishness like that," her mother stated matter-of-factly. "What kind of parent could agree with something like that?"

"Rolland said his mother —"

"Oh, Roxanne, please," she said in the dry tone. "This is a closed subject."

"Well, if that's a closed one, can I bring up something else?" Roxanne thought she'd ask.

"It depends," said her mother, "if it's something worth my discussing."

"It's worth it to me," Roxanne told her.

"Well, I want to hear then," her mother said.

"You know how you say I can't have anyone in the house until you're home?"

"Yes."

"Well I'm in junior high now. And it's kind of embarrassing to tell people this."

"Did you understand before why I felt it was important?" asked her mother.

"Yes, I sorta understood that. Anything could have happened, like you said. But now . . ."

"I guess you have a point," her mother responded before she could finish. "You *are* older. And you've shown that you can be trusted. I guess it would be all right. But only girls! You hear?"

"Now what boy would I have in here, Mommie?" she asked, looking up from her dinner and laughing.

"Well, there's the obvious Rolland!" her mother replied.

"Oh, Mommie!" Roxanne said, throwing up her hand. "Nobody wants to believe me when I tell them Rolland's in another world."

It turned out that quite a few people stayed home from school on Halloween. Mrs. Weisbaum had the same look of disgust on her face that Roxanne's mother had had the evening before. She obviously thought that it was ridiculous for kids to stay out on Halloween! Roxanne was glad she had shown up.

At this point, she still couldn't figure out just what

the big scare was supposed to be! Nothing seemed any different to her this morning.

As the day went on, little changed. Roxanne noticed that quite a few boys were walking around with weird stuff like overalls half done at the top. And some had one pant leg rolled up and the other leg down. A few girls had on mixed-matched socks and shoes. But weird as these things were, they were things she had seen kids wear on normal days! So she couldn't blame this part of the scene on Halloween!

No one was *acting* any crazier than usual either. Unless she wanted to count the cook in the cafeteria, who got the bright idea of coloring rice orange! Cafeteria rice was gummy enough as it was. The food coloring made it even more disgusting! The faces that kids made when they saw it, were about the most Halloweenish thing Roxanne had seen at school all day!

Up until she returned to afternoon homeroom, she was thinking, Rolland got some false information. Because Halloween ain't saying a thing unusual here!

But then when school ended, she walked dead into Nut City! There were groups of kids (some of whom she had never seen in school before) running around outside. They were throwing water balloons and, yes, *good eggs*!

Margarita and N.E. were laughing like they wanted to hang around. But Roxanne threw a quick wave to them, and then to Pat, and took off!

She squeezed her way onto the first bus that came along. Looking around, she hoped to see someone that she halfway knew. Sharon from the projects. Boobie. One of the cleaning ladies. Anybody! It didn't matter. She just wanted one familiar person to stand next to, with so many kids bugging out. But Roxanne didn't see a soul. As she inched along, she was pushed several times just for brushing up against someone. It didn't matter that the bus was crowded. Some kids automatically shoved you when you brushed up against them accidently. Trying her best not to touch anyone else, she bent down and pulled her body in.

"Watch out!" someone shouted as one of the water balloons came flying across the bus! It barely missed Roxanne. The boy that it landed on was fussing and pushing to see if he could get to the person who had thrown it.

A boom box blasted from the back, while the driver shouted for it to be turned off. At one point the driver stopped the bus altogether, and threatened not to move until the boom blasting ended. The troublemakers stopped playing the music, but then began picking at the bus driver. He shouted back at them word for word.

Roxanne was about ready to get off and try to walk the rest of the way home, when the bus stopped to pick up what looked like one of the maids. She had never seen this particular lady before. The woman got on carrying two full shopping bags. She was tall and lean, and wore her silver hair pulled back in a tight bun. The woman frowned as she began making her way through the bus, shopping bags and all. Veins popped up in her neck as she took note of the commotion.

"What kind of foolishness is going on here?" she shouted, midway in the bus. "Stop cuttin' the fool and act like you got home training!" she ordered, sounding like the mother of all!

At first there were a few chuckles — the kind of nervous laughter people let out when they're not sure if something is supposed to be funny or not.

To Roxanne, it was as if kids were trying to wait and see if this woman was playing with a full deck! After all, she'd had nerve to take them on. But as the lady continued, it became clear that she was no weird shopping-bag lady! She may have been loaded down like one, but she was fully sane!

"Your mothers and fathers would want to disown you if they saw you out here carrying on like this!" she shouted. "You put them to shame, acting this way!"

Her words bounced across the bus, hitting the

troublemakers in the right spot. The lady let them know that their behavior said something about their parents! And no matter what the real deal at home was, everybody wanted you to believe they came from the best. Roxanne smiled, as the bus got quiet.

The driver looked over his shoulder, smiling, too.

He handled it all wrong, Roxanne began thinking. When kids started calling him names, he called them names back, sounding all wack just like them! The lady was cool though, breaking everything down the way she did. 'Igging her would be like saying, you had raggedy roots!

CHAPTER 12

Margarita and N.E. had finally gotten the attention of their dream boys, Malik and Thad. And nobody could touch them! They had ended up saying something to the guys first. But still, they were talking with them at last! So Roxanne was sticking with Kenya and Pat. It ended up being mostly Pat, with Kenya out so much.

With all the time Roxanne had spent with Pat, she still knew no more about her. Or Kenya! When she finally asked Pat for her phone number one day, Pat awkwardly told her that she would have to call Kenya. Roxanne wasn't sure what that meant. She guessed that Pat had some special house rules about talking on the phone. She really didn't know. Because the girl had yet to call her. But someone *new* had!

An eighth-grade boy named Marcus was calling her. She didn't really like him *that* much. But after Margarita's smart remark about her needing to get a life, she told Marcus, "Yes," that he could call her at home. Then she'd quickly passed him her phone number in the hallway. And he had been calling her ever since.

The way it all started was that Marcus kept watching her on her way to gym class every day. Then one day he walked up and told her that he knew somebody who liked her.

"Who?" she asked innocently.

"Me!" he said. And that got the ball rolling.

Margarita and N.E. congratulated her on having a guy to talk with. But it didn't get Roxanne back into their lunch set. The boys they knew were both in seventh grade. So they made a foursome every day now.

Marcus had a different lunch period from Roxanne. But even if he hadn't, she wanted to believe that she wouldn't have dropped Kenya and Pat, like Margarita and N.E. had dropped *everybody*!

When Roxanne first told Maxine that an eighth-grader was talking to her, Maxine wanted to know if she was sure that she was ready for someone that age!

Roxanne asked, "What you mean, *that age*? The boy's only fourteen and I'll be thirteen on my birthday!"

Then Maxine got into a whole thing about him actually being almost two years older!

Roxanne figured that Maxine was probably upset

that she'd done something to top her for a change! Maxine hadn't mentioned a thing lately about the cute Harlem Boys' Choir guy she'd met the first of the year. The only person Roxanne heard her talking about now was the same-ole-same-ole Boobie! The Max had this new thing where she wanted everybody to refer to Boobie by his real name, Clarence! Roxanne told her that she'd try, but that in her heart-of-hearts the boy would always be Boobie!

She made a mistake, telling Maxine that Marcus had asked to come by her house after school to study. Though Maxine knew fully well that she was just now getting permission to let *her* in, she'd had nerve to think she didn't know any better than to try to let Marcus stop by!

"Girl, you know that I'm not that crazy!" Roxanne told her.

"You have to watch out for those older guys though!" Maxine warned. "They'll try to psyche you out!"

Roxanne really didn't know why Maxine talked to her like she was so green. Even if she was dumb enough to want to try something like sneaking a guy *in*, there was her father to worry about. He was always popping up unexpectedly. All she needed, was to have him come by and catch her in the wrong!

One day recently, he *had* dropped by briefly.

When Roxanne let her father in, she was on the phone with Marcus. As her dad took a seat, she kept talking for a few minutes. Not particular about him knowing that a boy was on the other end, she neatly switched the conversation to a school subject. But her father wasn't fooled.

"Who was that?" he asked, as soon as she hung up.

"A friend," Roxanne answered, hoping that would do.

"What kind of friend?" he wanted to know.

"A good one!" she felt like saying. But her father didn't have the kind of look on his face that said he was playing with her.

When he found out that it was a boy, he began rubbing his chin and looking all serious. Roxanne braced herself for a lecture.

Her father started up with comments about her homework being the most important thing for her to concentrate on after school. "I'm not trying to say that you shouldn't have friends," he added. "But you have to focus on your schoolwork first! These are crucial years. If you slip on your grades now, it'll be hard to catch up later."

"Daddy, I do my homework," she told him.

"Does *do* mean you haven't *done* it today?" he asked.

"I haven't *done* it yet today," she had to admit,

"but I *do* it. And I even spend time in the library at school studying," she pointed out.

"What happened to Rolland?" her father asked next.

"Daddy, I can't go through junior high with just Rolland for a friend!" she told him.

"I understand, baby," he said. "It's just that I know Rolland. And I know that he's a nice boy. This Marcus may be, too. Time will tell."

Roxanne didn't pay much attention to her father's words at the time he spoke them. But it was the very next day that Marcus brought up the business about coming to her house after school.

"You won't be the first person not to follow every rule their parents make," Marcus said, trying to convince her that it was no big deal.

As much as Roxanne hated to let Maxine in on it, she *had* to tell somebody! One thing Maxine said on the subject kept coming back to her.

"He might be testing you," she suggested.

"Testing me how?" Roxanne asked.

"Just *seeing* if you'll do something wrong," Maxine explained. "Remember the time Dottie Lawson tried to push us all up to steal a piece of bubble gum from the deli?"

"Yeah," Roxanne recalled. "You and I had the good sense not to take a piece!"

"But ole stupid go-along Ebony took it and got

caught!" said Maxine. "And all the while, Dottie stood there never taking a piece herself! Then after Ebony gets caught, Dottie goes around the projects spreading the news!"

"When she was the one who had pushed her up to do it!" Roxanne added.

"Now you get my drift, homegirl?" Maxine ended.

And Roxanne certainly did.

Lying across her bed now, with a Keith Sweat tape playing, she rolled all this around in her head: The Max could be right. I could allow Marcus to push me up to let him in my house when I shouldn't. Then he could go around telling people. And next thing I know, everybody'll be whispering about me! I'm not saying that he would necessarily do this. But he could!

Roxanne had never told Margarita and N.E. about Marcus asking to come by after school. This part of her business, she was keeping completely from those two! Because she wanted them to make a fuss over her talking to an eighth-grade boy for as long as possible. It was such a thrill the first time Margarita and N.E. saw her with Marcus. He had walked her to gym class that day. Margarita was the first one to spot the two of them.

"GOOOONE girl!" she said, snapping her finger and making a circle in the air, once Marcus turned to leave. Then she'd rushed to get N.E. to come see before Marcus was out of sight.

"How you rate an eighth-grader?" Margarita wanted to know.

"Never mind him being an eighth-grader," said N.E. "How she get one so cute?"

"Yeah," said Margarita. "How you do that?"

"I didn't *do* anything," Roxanne replied. "He said something to me first. The same way somebody might have with you two if you hadn't been so anxious!"

" 'Scuse me, Mis' Thang!" N.E. snapped. "I'll admit that I was the first one to say something to Thad. But for your information, he said he had eyes on me all along!"

"Anyhow, these the nineties, girlfriend!" Margarita fired at her. "A female can speak up first if she feel like it! Besides, the average seventh-grade boy happens to be pretty shy. It takes a while for them to warm up to girls."

Roxanne had to admit that Margarita was right about the last part. She'd seen it happening all around with seventh-grade girls and guys. The boys *were* getting bolder as the year went on! Just the other day, Countrytime, of all people, came sneaking up behind her whispering, "Hi, sweetie!" Then before she had a chance to tell him off, he took off running down the hall!

CHAPTER 13

Roxanne thought she'd never get a chance for Rolland to see her with Marcus. It finally happened one day after school. Marcus was walking her to the bus stop, carrying her books. She was so happy when she saw Rolland up ahead. He was alone for a change.

Lately, everywhere she turned she saw him and Jewel! She'd seen the two walking down the hall one day *holding hands*! There was a sign up against that. So they would have been in big trouble had a teacher come along. Roxanne figured it was one thing to get that friendly outside, but as the principal had said, some people went too far in the building!

Well, Rolland can get his eyes full now! she told herself as they reached where he was standing. She was sorry that the bus was coming and they couldn't linger a while longer.

Surprising herself as much as she suspected she did Marcus, Roxanne reached over and patted the top of his head. Then he shocked her back with a kiss on the cheek! She was so nervous she almost dropped the books he was passing to her.

"Later, Luv," Marcus said all cool and well in range of Rolland's ears! Roxanne was sure that she was red, as the blood rushed to her head. This was so perfect, she thought. All the times I've passed Rolland, watching him look all lovey-dovey at Jewel. Well, now it's *my* turn!

She boarded the bus, knowing that Rolland was dead on her trail. There were no seats left, so she grabbed a pole.

"May I stand by you, *Luv*?" Rolland asked, laughing as he said it.

Roxanne was cool, simply smiling and moving over without commenting on his smart remark. All that mattered to her was that they were even now!

"Why didn't you tell me that you had a new friend?" he asked.

"I didn't know I was supposed to be reporting to you," Roxanne replied. "Where's Jewel this afternoon?"

"I hafta have my space," he said, trying to be all hip.

"There sure wasn't any space between you the other day," Roxanne cracked. "I couldn't believe that you all were walking down the hall holding hands!"

"Well, look who's talking!" he cried. "*Luv*, who got kissed at the bus stop!"

"Oh, you're just jealous!" she said.

"Yeah, maybe I am!" he said, to her surprise.

She tried not to blush, but felt it happening anyhow. Maaan, she thought. Everything's going so smooth for me! Wait 'til I tell Maxine!

Marcus called her as soon as she got home. "I *really* wanted to follow you all the way today!" he crooned in her ear.

Roxanne thought, Uh-oh. He's gonna start on that again! He surprised her though by switching to another subject. But then it turned out to be one that was just as aggravating.

He wanted her to ask for permission to go to the movies one Saturday evening!

"I remember what you said your mother had to say about girls your age dating," Marcus told her. "So don't call it a date. Just say that you're going to meet some friends there. And then I'll hook up with you," he said, laying out the whole plan.

"But I've never gone to the movies in the evening," she tried explaining.

"I'm talking early evening!" he said. "It's not even dark at six o'clock! Don't you know some girl who could come with you? I could ask another guy."

"I don't know," Roxanne said, stalling, which she knew made no sense. There was a better chance of it snowing in July, than there was of her getting permission to go to the movies at night!

She called and told Maxine about it later — and how Marcus kept naming other girls from school he'd seen at the movies in the evening.

"I told you he would try to psyche you out!" Maxine reminded her. "He's trying to make you think you're the only person in the world who can't go out at night. And believe me, not too many girls our age are in the movies after five!"

"You're in there!" Roxanne pointed out.

"That's because I'm supposed to be going with my sister. That's what my mother thinks when we leave. We break up afterward."

"Hmph. Hmph!" Roxanne uttered. "And you're not just going to the movies alone with Boobie like I've been thinking?"

"Not really," she said. "My mother just started letting my *sister* date. So you know she's not about to let me!"

"I don't know what I'm going to do," Roxanne said pitifully.

"Just tell that ole Marcus how I-S is!" Maxine spelled out. "And if he can't deal with it, say later!"

"I guess," Roxanne said slowly. Maxine made it all sound so easy, but it wasn't. It would probably mean the end of Marcus's phone calls, she figured. And Margarita and N.E. would start saying "get a life" all over again. There would be no more strutting past Rolland either!

But there would also be no more aggravation, she thought further. No more of him worrying me about coming by my house. And now, going to the movies . . .

Later, when her mother came in, Roxanne stood around in the kitchen while she cooked.

"What's wrong?" her mother turned and asked at a point.

"I'm okay," Roxanne said, bothered that her mother had picked up her vibes.

"You don't look like you're okay. But if you don't talk to me, I can't help," her mother indicated.

"I'm okay," Roxanne repeated. Then she got up to leave. She needed to go and hide. Her mother knew her too well. And Roxanne knew that if she stayed in the kitchen much longer, her mother would pull everything out that she was trying *not* to say.

She wished that she could talk with her mother about Marcus. But she wasn't sure how she would take it.

Over the summer, she and her mother had what she and Maxine called, The Famous Boy Talk. It started out with a long speech on how so many young girls around the projects were "getting in trouble." There were three steps that led to trouble, according to her mother: Number one was holding hands with a boy. Number two was kissing. And number three, was him touching your knee.

Roxanne felt embarrassed throughout the whole talk. But she'd been warned by Maxine that it was surely coming. With Maxine having an older sister, she got the talk earlier along with her sister, and she had passed it all on to Roxanne. Of course they'd both read much more than their mothers realized. Not to mention all they'd seen on TV. So there was little that was new to them in this conversation.

Roxanne's mother had ended her session, saying that there was a good time yet before she had to be concerned about dating boys. But that she wasn't too young to have the information. Especially since someone in the projects, only twelve years old, had "gotten into trouble."

After the talk, she asked Roxanne if she had any questions. She'd answered no. Like most people her age, she knew about the birds and the bees. And like *everybody* living in the projects, she knew about the babies having babies. But as far as she was concerned, this had *nothing* to do with her! However, her mother obviously didn't see it that way.

So where was she to begin now? Her mother might tell her not to let *anybody* in the house, if she brought up anything . . . not even Maxine.

CHAPTER 14

"Check out Miss Roxanne's report card!" Margarita said as N.E. walked up behind them in the hallway. They had just been dismissed from homeroom.

"Don't ask to see mine!" cried N.E.

"Come on, you gotta!" Roxanne said, pulling at her.

"No! No," she screamed, hiding behind Margarita, whose embarrassing card Roxanne had seen in afternoon homeroom.

"Let's go," Margarita said to N.E.

"Can't you all wait five minutes after school anymore?" asked Roxanne. "I wanted to talk to you again about the study group idea," she said, thinking this was a good time to bring it up.

Kiku and her friends had a group that met in the library two or three times a week. Obviously Roxanne was biting somebody else's idea. But she figured, so what? It was something worth copying. Who would care if she stole it?

"I still say we oughta get together sometimes during lunch as a group," Roxanne said.

"Girlfriend, *pluuueze*," Margarita said, rocking her head from side to side and rolling her eyes toward the sky.

"Well, you see what studying got me," Roxanne bragged, holding up her report card.

"I guess she did good, too, huh?" N.E. said, referring to Pat who passed, waving good-bye to them.

"Who wouldn't have good grades if they kept their nose stuck in a book as much as she does!" Margarita said. "And it goes for this one, too," she added, turning and facing Roxanne.

"All I know is that you can't get no more than you work for," Roxanne responded smugly. "And you, Margarita, how can *anybody* end up with a D in Mr. Hill's class?"

"I hate how he never sticks to the subject!" she said.

"Sure doesn't," N.E. agreed.

"That's what makes it interesting," Roxanne tried to tell them. She was amazed at how differently they saw this from her. "I like Mr. Hill's style," she told them.

"That's 'cause you weird," cracked N.E.

"Studyin' at lunchtime," Margarita snapped.

"Yeah. You and that weird Pat," N.E. continued, laughing. "She ever tell you anything about whatever happened to our, or I should say *her*, disappearing friend Kenya?"

"No," Roxanne answered. "I keep hoping that one day I'll see Kenya's grandmother on the bus. But I haven't yet."

"Seems like Pat would tell you the story with you hanging with her almost every day. I agree with N.E. that she's one strange cookie all right," Margarita said.

"I can't figure you and N.E.," shouted Roxanne. "First I'm the fruitcake, then Pat!"

"Well both of you are peculiar!" said Margarita. "Like the other day. I saw Marcus come up when you were with Pat. She didn't have the smarts to get lost, and you went walking on to the library with her! I don't know many girls who would have done that!"

"I had to work on a book report. The kind of thing that got me these grades," Roxanne fired, waving the card again. "That's what Pat does a lot at lunchtime, too. Get in some extra studying!"

"She needs to do some extra shopping!" Margarita cracked, laughing. "I'm about too tired of seeing her in the same thing over and over."

"Wooord!" N.E. added, laughing along with Margarita.

"I can't believe you all!" Roxanne shouted, angrily. "Standin' around countin' what somebody wears! I got to go!"

"Wait!" N.E. called out to her. "There's something we almost forgot to tell you about."

"You're going to tell her?" Margarita asked, making a face.

"Tell me what?" Roxanne questioned.

"About a Jam," N.E. whispered. "There's gonna be one Friday."

"Friday when?" asked Roxanne.

"FRI-DAY!" N.E. sounded out. "This guy Thad knows, named Raheem, is having the party. Nobody's gonna be home at his house until late Friday night. So at lunchtime . . ."

"Lunchtime?" shouted Roxanne.

"Don't talk so loud," Margarita whispered.

"Yeah. It's a secret," said N.E. "The reason I didn't tell you before was because I knew you were gonna get all wide-eyed like you're doing."

"What kind of party can you have at lunchtime?" Roxanne wanted to know.

"It's just *starting* at lunchtime," N.E. explained. "Haven't you ever heard of a hooky party?"

"If you're too scared . . ." Margarita began.

"Lots of eighth-graders are going," said N.E. "Probably Marcus, too. But if you want him to think you're not down for the action, it's all right with us!"

"I didn't say that I wouldn't go. I just need to think about it," said Roxanne.

"Well, we've done *our* thinking and we're going!" Margarita announced. "And if you want to ever be in on what's going on, now's your chance to get started!"

Seeing Marcus walking in their direction, Margarita and N.E. grinned and made faces at each other. Then Margarita made a remark about the two of them knowing when it was time to go, *unlike* someone else!

Roxanne was glad that they were leaving. She wanted to ask Marcus alone just what he knew about this party! He hadn't said anything to her about it.

"Have you heard anything about a hooky party on Friday?" she asked when he reached her.

"Yeah!" he said, starting to walk alongside her. "I just heard about it. They say it's s'pose to be *large*, too!"

"Margarita and N.E. say they're going. And they're trying to get me to go," Roxanne told him.

"Oh, that'll be the move!" Marcus exclaimed. "I can introduce your homegirls to my homeboys. Then we can all hook up for the movies one Saturday like I wanna. You asked to go yet?"

"Not yet!" she answered, thinking, Daaag! In one breath you're telling me to cut class on Friday, and in another, to lie about going on a date with you. How many wrong things do you think I can concentrate on at one time?

Marcus started laying out the plan, telling her how he could write an excuse for her homeroom teacher. He had it all figured out, the same as he did the movie scheme. Yet she hadn't even said that she would definitely go! Daaag! she repeated to herself as he went on and on. She was glad when the bus came.

Riding home, she thought it all through. She didn't much care what Margarita and N.E. would say if she didn't go to the party. They had gone down the scale with her in the friendship department. It started with them dumping her every day at lunch. And now, this afternoon, they had called her weird! Plus they were snapping on Pat's clothes, like *they* were some fashion plates!

She was learning that people really did change. Just like her father had said. It was the reason he told her he and her mother broke up. That "people just change." Margarita and N.E. sure had. So she really didn't care what they had to say about her going, or not going. What she did care about though, were the cool people they said were going to be there. And the thought of missing all that! Then there was Marcus. She wanted him to see that she could do at least *one* thing! She knew she was not getting out of the house to go to any movie with him like he hoped. So she thought maybe she should go for it on Friday!

'Course there was the flip side: What if, for some reason, she got caught and her mother and father found out? They'd probably go into instant shock! She was sure they could never picture her doing something as outrageous as cutting school! Now if someone reported some *little* wrong, say like maybe hearing her curse, she figured her parents would be surprised, but they probably wouldn't dispute anybody that it was impossible. But to be told she'd cut school? She could picture them shaking their heads going, "NO! You must have the wrong person. Oh, no, not Roxanne!"

Later at home, while she was flipping between *Oprah* and *Donahue*, Rolland called. Roxanne was puzzled and wondered why he was calling her.

"So tell me more about your new boyfriend," he started off, all casually, like the two of them talked on the phone every afternoon.

"Do I get into your business, Rolland?" Roxanne snapped.

"What business?" he asked.

"Jewel business!" she said.

"That's history," Rolland told her.

"Oh, yeah," she said, ready to hear more.

"Yeah, we broke up for good," Rolland informed her.

"Whose good?" Roxanne joked.

"Oh, you know what I mean," he said.

"What happened?" Roxanne asked.

"Lots of stuff," Rolland began. "She got tired of me talking about you for one thing."

"Oh, plueeeze! Stop trying to jive me Rolland."

"For real," he said. "She got mad one day when she saw me talking to you."

"What day?"

"You were walking down the hall with a redhead girl."

"Pat!" she exclaimed. "I remember. All you did was speak to me!"

"I know!" he said. "It wasn't just you though. Any time I even smiled at another girl . . ."

"Really?" went Roxanne. "It's not that way with me and Marcus," she said, trying to sound like she had it all together.

"Well, that's cool," said Rolland. "I looked for you today after school. I guess you were with your guy, huh?"

"Actually I wasn't," she said. "I was wasting time with my suppose-to-be friends!"

"Suppose-to-be?" he asked.

"Well, they *are*, after dissing me this afternoon. They called me stupid for going to the library with Pat one day, when I could have gone with Marcus! They think you're suppose to put a boy before *everything!* They're the ones need to be going to the library to study, instead of trying to diss *me!*" she said.

"By the way, how you make out on your report card?" Rolland asked.

"Pretty good," Roxanne replied, not wanting to brag about her one A and five B's.

"I can do better," Rolland confessed. "Now that I'm back in the world again, maybe I can study more. Jewel wanted me to meet her every morning, eat with her every day, and ride home with her after school! I ran out of anything interesting to say!"

Roxanne thought, Rolland? Since when did he become concerned with whether or not what he had to say was interesting? He's *changing*, too!

"Maybe I'll come down some night after your mother's home. We can study together," he suggested.

"Maaaaybe," she said.

"Just maybe?" he asked, pressing his luck.

And she repeated it for him. "Maybe."

She did like the way Rolland had put the question though. Without her even saying so, he took for granted that he couldn't be in her house without her mother.

The one and only person she had let into the apartment so far, was ringing the doorbell now. "Who?" Roxanne called out, looking through the peephole.

"Whitney Houston!" she heard Maxine saying from outside. "Why you always asking who?" Maxine asked, as she let her in.

" 'Cause you could be anybody!" Roxanne explained.

"Yeah, like Whitney!" Maxine joked. "Here's the book I promised to bring," she said, passing Roxanne another sweep-away.

"Be sure not to let your mother find this one," Maxine warned. "My sister still doesn't know that one of her romances has been thrown in the trash!"

"I'll keep this one safe," Roxanne promised. "I tried to tell my mother the book didn't belong to me. But she threw it in the garbage anyway."

"Well, I won't deny that it may have been where it belonged," Maxine said, giggling. "Wait 'til you read the junk in this one!"

"My history teacher says that you learn something from *everything* you read!" Roxanne said, checking out the jacket of *Love Struck!*

"Yeah, a lot in there is educational all right," Maxine agreed. "The same as watching *Oprah* can be sometimes," she said, getting settled in front of the television.

"Guess who called me today?" Roxanne said.

"Who?" asked Maxine.

"Rolland! And he come asking if we could get together to study sometime in the evening!"

"I told you before that that's how it goes!" cried Maxine. "The minute a person sees that someone else is interested, suddenly they're more interested! Same thing with me and Clarence. Soon as he knew I knew a Harlem Boys' Choir singer, he was in my face every day!"

"I've just about decided that I don't want a main guy," Roxanne said. "We're too young to be so serious."

"Speak for yourself, hon!" Maxine kidded.

"Oh, yeah! I have something else to tell you." Roxanne suddenly remembered. "This *is* serious! Margarita and N.E., who I'm only semi-tight with these days, asked me about cutting on Friday to go to a hooky party!"

"You said no, didn't you?" Maxine said right away.

Roxanne answered slowly, "I wanted to, but Marcus is going and . . ."

"See what I meant about those older guys!" fired Maxine.

"Well, it's not just Marcus," Roxanne continued. "A lot o' cool people are supposed to be there."

"Have you thought about what you plan to do when the cut shows up on your report card?" Maxine asked her.

"That's a long ways off," Roxanne replied. "I could say the teacher made a mistake or something. I don't know. Marcus said he'd write me a note, saying that I had to leave school early that day."

"Homegirl, you need to slow down," Maxine advised. "What about your other friend? The one who's been away!"

"Talking about Kenya?" Roxanne asked.

"Yeah," she said.

"Kenya still didn't come back," Roxanne told her. "And none of us know what happened."

"I thought she hadn't," said Maxine. "Because she sounded like the one with the most sense in your group!"

"Excuse me," Roxanne said.

"Oh, I'm sorry." Maxine laughed. "The most sense next to you!"

"That's better!" Roxanne said.

"It takes a bold person to play hooky, Roxanne," Maxine stated.

"And you think I'm not?" she asked.

"Girlfriend, I wouldn't try it if anyone at school asked me to do something like it."

"Who at your school would be down for something like this anyhow?" Roxanne questioned.

"Oh, just because it's a private, doesn't mean everybody there is good," Maxine pointed out. "Some wack ones in the crowd there, too! What did Rolland say about this?"

"What makes you think I told him?" Roxanne said sharply.

"I just though you all were close again," Maxine explained.

"No closer than we ever were," Roxanne noted.

"Just remember what I said though, homegirl," Maxine ended. "You need to slow down."

CHAPTER 15

Roxanne could see that Rolland was back to his old tricks. Maybe he had watched from his front window. She didn't know, but somehow he'd managed to walk out of the building a few minutes after her the past two days.

"Can I carry your books?" he asked this morning, smiling widely.

"I got 'em," Roxanne said. She was glad that he wasn't stuck to Jewel like glue anymore. But still, she felt she needed to keep things between the two of them under control.

"Roxanne," he began. "I know you got a new guy."

New? she thought. Did I ever announce that you were the old one, Rolland?

"Ah, I . . ." Rolland struggled on, forcing her to help him out.

"So what's the problem?" she asked.

"I might as well tell you that I go crazy seeing you with that guy!" he blurted out.

"Oh, Rolland," she said, feeling embarrassed by

what he was saying. Embarrassed not just because he had said this to her, but from knowing that it was exactly how she had felt watching him stick with Jewel! But never, never, *never*, would she have admitted it to him, like he was 'fessing up to her!

"Maybe there shouldn't be no boyfriend/girlfriend thing at our age," she suggested, trying to make him feel better. "Maybe we all need to just be friends, with girls talking to different guys and vice versa."

"That way, somebody like Jewel won't have to be freaking out!" he cut in. " 'Course it shouldn't be *too* many friends now," Rolland kidded. "And I should definitely be one of the ones you close to," he ended, touching Roxanne's shoulder.

"Git outta here!" she said, pushing him away.

The bus had come.

"Oh, look!" Roxanne cried out, seeing who sat there, as they got on. It was Kenya's grandmother at last! Only seeing Kenya herself could have made Roxanne happier. "I have to speak to her!" she told Rolland.

"Who? What?" he asked, wondering what she was so excited about.

"That lady," Roxanne said, pointing. "I need to ask her something! I'll be right back."

"Ma'am," Roxanne said, once she reached her.

"Yes, baby," the woman answered softly, looking up with a smile.

"I am a friend — was a friend," Roxanne began, sounding all confused. "I knew your granddaughter Kenya. She was in my class. And me, and some of the girls who knew her, were wondering why she ain't come back."

The woman took on a worried expression. Starting off slowly, she asked, "How well you know Kenya?"

"Pretty good," Roxanne replied.

"Probably not as good as you thought," she said. "Kenya was only with me a little while. See, her family was burned out of their apartment. And they were shuffled from here to yonder. This city hotel to that one. Even the little while Kenya was with me, it was back and forth for the family. They finally are settled in a halfway decent apartment. I'm glad, because I know Kenya missed my other lil' grans. Kenya, she's the oldest. And almost like a little mother herself. She was a big help, staying home with the younger ones while me and her mama looked for a place. Seemed like it would take forever before we found something decent. Weeks it took."

"I guess that's why Kenya was out so much." Roxanne stated.

"That, and the fact that her mother has asthma. It seems to have gotten worse since she lost the children's father in the fire. He was trying to save the baby . . ."

"Oh! I'm so sorry," Roxanne said, feeling hurt for Kenya and her family as she heard this story.

"The teachers at school knew about everything," the woman continued. "They understood that Kenya was only with me until her family got an apartment. And like I said, it took some doing! But still, they luckier than some. Kenya has a friend whose family's been in a welfare hotel going on two years now. And the family's *white*, too! Shows that this happens to all kind of people. Hard times can hit anybody!"

"That's a long time to live in a hotel," Roxanne commented, remembering all the sad stories she'd seen on the news about people living in welfare hotels. Whole families cooped up together in one room, eating all their meals outside. One woman had told how she had fried chicken on a hot plate in their room, until the hotel owner caught her. Another lady told of using her iron to make grilled cheese sandwiches for her children. Roxanne wondered if Kenya had gone through anything like this.

"Yes, two years a *long* time to be in a welfare hotel," the woman was saying. "What's the chile's name? . . . Patricia!" she said, snapping her finger as it came to her. "Patricia Foxworth!" she ended, causing Roxanne to almost lose her balance where she stood. "Foxworth don't even sound like the name of anybody poor, does it?" she asked.

"Sur — sure doesn't," Roxanne managed to say. She came looking for Kenya's story and had discovered Pat's, too!

"Listen, honey," the woman said finally. "I'd just as soon have you say to your friends that I only told you Kenya moved. See, I wouldn't tell just anybody all that I told you. But I didn't mind giving you the whole story. Because to me, you got the kind of face that can be trusted."

"Don't worry," Roxanne assured her. She knew all too well that she couldn't breathe a word of it to anyone. Not when one of the persons in the story happened to still be around. "I'm glad I saw you," she said, about to leave. "I've been looking for you for the longest!"

"Oh, I only do half days up here now," the woman explained. "So I generally leave much later. Half a day is all the people I'm going to can afford. Like I said, hard times can hit anybody. They really can't even afford me half days. But they rather give up something less important, if you know what I mean."

"I think so," Roxanne said, smiling, over how much the woman reminded her of Kenya. Or is it suppose to be the other way around? she asked herself.

Rolland had his neck all stretched forward, waiting for information when she got back. But all he got out of her was what she'd said before. The lady was somebody she needed to speak to!

"Just act normal. Just act normal," Roxanne repeated over and over when she reached homeroom. Though she was still very much in shock, she didn't want a strange look on her face when she saw Pat.

"What's up?" she asked her, trying to greet Pat as lightly as she could.

"Nothing," her friend mumbled, glancing up from what she was reading.

"I saw Kenya's grandmother this morning," said Roxanne.

"What did she say?" Pat asked, closing the book now and laying it down.

"That Kenya moved," Roxanne answered, trying to look as natural as she could.

Margarita walked into the room just then. Roxanne was glad that she strolled on up front and didn't stop anywhere near them. Remembering what Margarita and N.E. had said yesterday about Pat's clothes, she got even angrier. What if *they* had to live in a welfare hotel? she thought. A crowded place with rats and roaches. If only they knew . . .

From the quiet way that Pat sat by her now, Roxanne worried that maybe she shouldn't have told her she'd seen Kenya's grandmother. Maybe she'd guessed that she knew more.

"Roxanne," Pat said, suddenly. "There's something I want to tell you! You promise it will just be between us?"

With a pretty good idea of what was coming, Roxanne promised.

"When you all were pushing to find out if I knew more about Kenya, I did. See, we used to live at the same place."

As Roxanne heard Pat's story, she discovered that it was worse than what Kenya's grandmother reported. Pat's younger sisters and brothers had been spread out in foster-care homes. And her mother and father were now separated.

While Roxanne couldn't relate to everything Pat was going through, she *could* identify with the girl's parents having broken up. So she cut in to share her own life, telling Pat how she cried for days after her father moved.

But as Pat went on, Roxanne saw that there was no real comparison here! Pat didn't even know where her father was anymore. Whereas in her own case, she was running around shopping and having a good time nearly every weekend with her dad. With nothing to compare, she kept her mouth shut from then on.

Pat talked and talked. Now that she was telling her story, it seemed she couldn't stop. Guess she's had it bottled up for so long, Roxanne was thinking.

"One hotel I stayed in was so far downtown that we had to take a bus to school," she said to Roxanne. "It was bad enough living at a hotel. But then *everybody* at school saw you getting off the welfare bus. And the hotel where I'm staying now, we have to share the bathroom with two other families on the same floor. It's horrible. Kids are always making noise. And parents arguing. I could never explain just how awful it is."

Mrs. Weisbaum was asking for volunteers to come up and be part of a seventh-grade activity committee being formed between the different homeroom classes. Laquita was the first one to jump up. And Margarita followed. There was talk going on about a monthly after-school dance. Roxanne wondered how Margarita could sit herself up there looking innocent and planning for what Mrs. Weisbaum had called some *wholesome* activities. She'd said without a doubt that she was going to the *un-wholesome* hooky party the next day.

Roxanne listened to Pat telling her that a social worker was talking about putting her in a group home for teenage girls. "If my mother's problem doesn't end soon," she said. She didn't tell Roxanne what the problem was. And Roxanne wasn't sure that she wanted to know. She'd heard so much of the girl's business already!

Pat told her how she and Kenya first met at the welfare hotel. When they met again at Riverdale Junior High, they made a pact to keep their homes a secret.

"Since Kenya's gone," Pat had stated sadly, "I don't mind telling you."

Roxanne let her go on, never letting on that she already knew some of what she was sharing.

"I'm sure people must guess that something's strange about me," Pat continued, nervously pushing the book back and forth across the desk. "Now you know why I couldn't give you a phone number. And these clothes I wear . . ."

"Pat, it's *who* you are that matters, not what you're wearing," Roxanne said, sounding like her mother.

"I guess," Pat said, sighing deeply. "I spoke to Mrs. Weisbaum about a baby-sitting job, and she's suppose to be telling someone about me."

"Sounds cool," said Roxanne.

When homeroom ended, Roxanne told Pat to be sure to look for her at lunchtime today. She was supposed to get together with Margarita and N.E. and give them a definite yes or no about the party, but she figured it could wait. Pat needed her.

Besides, she didn't really have an answer for Margarita and N.E. anyhow. And she would spend the rest of the morning struggling to come up with one.

She was sorry now that they'd ever let her in on the stupid party!

"What's with you today, young lady?" Mr. Hill asked at a point in history class where he noticed that she wasn't participating as usual.

"Ah, I . . . I was just daydreaming," Roxanne confessed.

"Well, that much is clear," he said, smiling. "Would you like to share your thoughts with us?" he asked. "They're obviously more interesting than ours, from the expression on your face."

"I heard everything!" Roxanne began. "All about the way schools were for African-American children in the South before integration. But I disagree with what Jason said. He said that African-American children were poorly educated under segregation. That's not all true.

"I know, because my mother went to segregated schools in Georgia. And she told me how it was. They did get leftover textbooks, desks, and other old things, while the white schools got *everything* new. And their buildings were never as nice. But there were always good teachers! So they were taught well. Martin Luther King, Jesse Jackson, my mother, and a whole lot of other important people went to segregated schools in the South!" Roxanne ended her speech, with all eyes in the classroom on her.

"That's why discussions like this are so important!" Mr. Hill said, walking back to his desk. "Class, Jason gave us the understanding he had from reading the history of segregation. And what Roxanne has done is bring a more personal point of view to the subject. So it comes back to what I'm always telling you! There is more history than you can get from between the pages of books!" he said. "Along with reading, you should talk to your parents. Your grandparents, too, if you can."

Roxanne's attention stayed with Mr. Hill and her classmates for a while longer. But soon, she was thinking of the party again. It was still on her mind when the period ended.

Then on her way to the next class, who did she pass and overhear talking about the party, but the Doorknockers?

They going? she thought with disgust. Are they supposed to be some of the cool people Margarita and N.E. claim gon' be there? Daaag! I certainly hope not. For they some of the last girls at school that I want to get to know better!

After worrying all morning, Roxanne never came any closer to deciding what she should do. Standing near the cafeteria and waiting for Pat, she looked up and saw Rolland coming down the hall! Turning sideways to pretend that she didn't see him was a waste of time.

"Watcha doing for lunch?" Rolland asked when he reached her. "Want to go up to Angelo's for pizza?"

"Not today," she told him flatly.

"You hear about this hooky party everybody's rappin' 'bout?" Rolland asked. "I hear a lot of people are cuttin' out 'round this time tomorrow. Even though I know you're not that crazy . . ."

"I'll see you later, Rolland," she said, to rush him along. "I'm waiting for a friend."

"Okay!" he said. "I know how to take a hint." Then winking at her, he backed away, snapping his fingers and sounding like an oldies tape as he sang. "Some-day, we'll be — togeeeether! Yes-we-will. Yes-we-will . . ."

Roxanne couldn't help laughing over his silliness. But as soon as he was out of sight, her expression changed. Daag, she thought, worrying. I wish he didn't know about the party. It makes thinking about going even harder!

Margarita and N.E. walked up before Pat got there. They were not alone though. Malik and Thad were by their sides. Roxanne was about to walk over to them, until Margarita made a face that said, "Get lost!"

Well, later for both o' y'all! Roxanne said to herself. All I wanted to do was say that I was *still think-ing* about tomorrow!

Margarita was pulling at Malik's arm. Stopping outside the cafeteria, the four of them began hitting at one another — the way Roxanne had watched them do so many times before. She guessed that this was supposed to be what people called love licks! Whatever it was, it looked real stupid to her! Margarita and N.E. were both giggling and punching at their particular guy, who was laughing and darting back and forth to dodge the licks.

Finally, Pat came. As she walked up to Roxanne, Margarita and N.E. stopped passing love licks long enough to look over at them. Then whispering to each other, they began laughing.

Sticks and stones may break my bones, but words will never hurt me, Roxanne said to herself. But she didn't really mean it. She *was* hurt over the way Margarita and N.E. had changed up and started act-ing funny.

Later on in afternoon homeroom, Margarita was still ignoring Roxanne. She had taken a seat along-side Laquita and Shanika, who seemed overjoyed that Margarita was back-in-friends with them again.

Pitiful's what it is, Roxanne thought, shaking her head over the situation. Margarita's got them fooled that she's somebody special. Somebody cool!

She figured that Margarita was probably telling

them about the party — which didn't seem to be a big secret around school. She had heard some more girls talking about it in the rest room that afternoon.

Roxanne knew that Marcus was probably going to be outside, waiting for an answer about the party. She hoped she could dodge him today.

Once they were dismissed, she tried to make a rush for the bus before Marcus came along. But just as she started off, she heard N.E. calling her from behind.

Roxanne was surprised to see both N.E. and Margarita walking to catch up with her. While N.E. hurried, Margarita more or less crept along. It was as though Margarita wasn't that particular about catching up with her at all. Finally N.E. began pulling Margarita by the arm.

"Margarita say you didn't say nothing to her about whether you're going or not," N.E. said after they'd reached her.

"She never asked!" snapped Roxanne.

"Well *'scuse me for livin', Mis' Thang*!" fired Margarita. "I didn't think we had to run you down to find out. Besides, what was I suppose to do? Come and talk in front of Pat."

"She knows how to keep a secret!" Roxanne stated. "Besides, it's not a secret anyhow! I heard some girls in the hallway talking about it! And some girls in the rest room."

"We tried to tell you that it's hot!" shouted N.E.

"Well, I didn't make up my mind yet," Roxanne told them.

"Come on!" Margarita snapped. "Why are we wasting precious time?"

"Roxanne!" she heard now, and looked and saw Marcus coming.

"Daaag!" she uttered once more.

"See you later," N.E. said, all cutesy. And Margarita simply made a face as they walked away.

"Why did you leave me?" Marcus asked, gasping to catch his breath from running. "You know I said to wait for me in the front."

"I forgot," she lied.

"So you ready for tomorrow?" he asked.

"I told you yesterday that I have to think about it some more!" she said.

"Well, if you don't know by now . . ." he began.

"I still have time," she told him, glad to see her bus waiting. "I have to go!" Roxanne ran off, leaving him looking confused. She knew that he expected her to stand around a few more minutes and talk. But she didn't need him pressuring her!

The girls from the rest room who had been talking about the party were on the same bus. And they were worse than the Doorknockers, it seemed to Roxanne. The Doorknockers were loud and silly, but she hadn't heard them use the language these girls were speaking. They sound gross! she told herself, wondering, Are *they* more of the cool ones? Shoot! I don't know if I wanna be seen at that thing tomorrow or not!

CHAPTER 16

"Roxanne! You're going to be late!" her mother shouted, walking toward her room.

"I'm leaving now!" she said, stopping to take one more look at herself. She still hadn't made up her mind, but she wanted to look perfect today, just in case she did go to the party.

"Well!" her mother exclaimed, stretching her eyes as she saw what she was wearing. "And where did *that* come from?" she asked about the new outfit Roxanne had on.

"I thought I showed you everything Daddy let me buy on Saturday," Roxanne said, stretching the truth.

"Girl, you know good and well that this is the first time I've seen this number you have on! There's no way I could have forgotten it! Turn around and let me see how this thing looks from behind!" her mother ordered, twirling her around.

"Mommie, it's what everybody's wearing," Roxanne said of the spandex skirt and tights set she wore. It was neon green on one side and black on the other.

"It looks like something you'd exercise in," her mother commented. "Did your father see you in this?"

"He didn't see me in any of the things I picked out! He lets me buy what I like!" Roxanne smartly remarked.

"Don't try to get fresh with me!" her mother said. "I bet he paid good money for that, too!" she said, still looking on with disapproval. "He has to stop letting you get anything you ask for," she continued. "I saw that dungaree jacket that you acted like you couldn't live without on the floor last week!" Then noticing the sad expression coming over her daughter's face, she spread her arms and cooed in baby talk, "Oh, come give Mommie a hug."

Roxanne stood still, refusing to move. If her mother wanted to make up, she was going to have to come to her side of the room!

"I'm sorry," her mother apologized, walking over and pulling her close. "I didn't mean to hurt your feelings."

"Now you have me thinking I don't look right!" Roxanne cried.

"I'm your mother, honey," she told her rocking Roxanne from side to side as she spoke. "It's my job to worry about how you look."

And-what-I-do! And-where-I-go! And-when-I-talk! Roxanne thought in silence — getting angrier as she remembered her mother telling her it was time to hang up the phone last night! She was sure that Marcus heard on the other end. It had been so *embarrassing*! She broke away from her mother's grip. "I'm no baby and I wish she would stop treating me like one!" she mumbled to herself, walking back over to the mirror for another look.

"I don't want you to leave feeling bad," her mother said, coming over and tugging at her skirt. "You need to pull that down just a little bit more."

"I have to go now!" Roxanne snapped impatiently.

"All right. Why don't I make shrimp tonight?" her mother suggested, knowing this was her daughter's favorite dish.

That's enough to let her off the hook, Roxanne thought, smirking as she gathered her books. She can diss mean all she wanna, if it means she has to end up making shrimp!

"See you later," her mother said, pulling at Roxanne's skirt once more before she walked out the door.

"Mommie, that's the way it's suppose to be!" Roxanne argued, twisting it back like she wanted it.

"I don't know," her mother said, shaking her head. "If that's what's groovy . . ."

"Mommie, ain't nothing *groovy* no more," Roxanne said heading on. "It's 'live!'"

"Whooa!" Rolland said,when she got downstairs. *"Roxanne! Roxanne!"*

"What are you still doing here?" she asked, blushing.

"Waiting for you. What else?" he said. "That outfit's baaad, Roxanne!"

"Thanks," she said, smiling and feeling better about what she was wearing. She started getting a little uncomfortable though, when two boys passed and stared longer than she thought was necessary. She had pulled the skirt up shorter after getting on the elevator. Maybe too short! she thought now, easing it back down some.

"Like I was saying to you yesterday," Rolland began after they were on the bus, "all these people are cutting today."

"Yeah," she said, shrugging her shoulders.

"I didn't want to say anything to you about it before. But I overheard your friend Marcus and some guys talking about going."

"So?" she went.

"So I worry," he said. "Because I know that you two are tight," Rolland continued. "And sometimes, depending on who you hang with . . ."

"Rolland, git outta here," she said, trying to throw him off. "Marcus is okay."

"If you say so," he said, leaving it alone.

Marcus was waiting where the bus stopped at school. Roxanne hated being in Rolland's face and all, now that he had told her how it hurt. But then, what could she do? She never told him to start waiting downstairs every day. And Marcus just happened to be there this morning! Rolland was cool though. Throwing up a hand, he waved good-bye and walked on.

"Here," Marcus said, passing a piece of paper to Roxanne.

"What's this?" she asked, opening up the folded sheet.

"Your excuse!" he said, grinning.

Roxanne smiled, too, when she looked and saw how he had "appointment" spelled all wrong!

"What's so funny?" he asked.

"Oh, just your writing the teacher telling her I have to go to the doctor this afternoon," she replied.

"Well, like I explained. I think it's cooler than just splitting," Marcus said, grinning some more. "See, I look out for you."

OH, suuure! she thought. With this dumb note! And I mean *dumb*! If you think I'm handing this thing to Mrs. Weisbaum you're crazy!

"So like me and my homies are leaving a lil' earlier than everybody else," Marcus was saying, his body rocking to the rhythm of his words. "Gonna try to get a few brews!" he leaned over and whispered.

"What?" she shouted. "People are going to be drinking?"

"Oh, not me!" Marcus said, slapping his palm across his chest, then raising it to the sky. "Honestly," he said. "I don't drink beer. But some people . . ."

"Marcus, I'm not going to this thing," she stated, balling up the note on the spot.

"Why?" he asked.

"You just reminded me of what happens at parties like this one. I know what time it is!"

"But you didn't say any of this before!" he said.

"I kept sayin' I wasn't sure!" she pointed out. "Now I am!"

"But you'll miss so much fun!" he said, pulling at her arm. "We gon' be jammin'!" he sang, still holding onto her and starting to dance around crazily. "And boogying and boogying, and boogying . . ."

"Stooop!" she shouted, breaking away.

"That's real 'live what you're rocking," Marcus said, checking her out as she stepped back.

"My mother's not too crazy about it," she stated, tugging at her skirt as she spoke.

"See, that's part of your problem," suggested Marcus. "You can't stop worrying about what your MAMA thinks! And she won't even let you talk on the phone after eight!"

"I told you before Marcus not to be saying anything bad about my mother!"

"I'm only putting into words what *you* think," he said.

"Just don't be talking about her," Roxanne ordered.

"You don't have to be embarrassed because she's old-fashioned," Marcus cracked.

"Boy, you don't even know my mother!" she fired, about ready to throw his misspelled note in his face! "I'd better go."

"Just *don't* say no!" Marcus shouted, making a joke out of it as she started to leave. "If you don't go, you'll make me look uncool to my homies!"

Like I care? she thought, walking on and dropping his note in the first trash can she passed.

"Margarita!" Roxanne called out, seeing her ahead.

"What?" Margarita turned and asked, looking annoyed.

"Wait!" she shouted, running. "I have something to tell you!"

"Don't tell me that you finally made up your mind!" Margarita said as she walked up.

"I'm not going!" Roxanne told her, huffing and puffing to catch her breath. "Marcus said that some guys are getting beer to take there!"

"How does he know?" Margarita asked.

"All I know is that I'm not being around any kids drinking beer!" Roxanne stated. "Anything could happen. Don't you watch the news?"

"Look, Roxanne," Margarita began, with her hand on her hip. "I told you in the beginning that if you weren't down for the thing, to keep yourself here! I tried to tell N.E. that you weren't ready! So why don't you just go on wherever-it-is you find to go at lunchtime, and just forget it! 'Cause I'm too tide o' you!" she ended with her famous hand wave.

"Well 'scuse *me* for living!" Roxanne said, throwing Margarita's line at her. "You don't have to jump all salty about it!"

"Wishy-washy people get on my nerves!" Margarita uttered walking on.

"Well, I wishy-washy I hadn't said anything to you about it!" Roxanne told her, knowing that she sounded ridiculous! She just wasn't good at matching anybody word for word.

"Don't think Marcus is going to keep talking to

someone who's not with it," Margarita warned.

"I don't haaardly care!" Roxanne informed her. "Because Marcus is *really* not my type!"

"Like you got a list!" Margarita joked, laughing.

"I'm not thinking about you, Margarita," Roxanne said, lost for words to keep up.

"And you *know* I'm not thinking about you!" Margarita shot back, determined not to be outdone, as they reached homeroom.

"What was that all about?" Pat asked when Roxanne sat beside her.

"Oh, nothing," she uttered.

"What's that you're reading?" Pat asked, seeing a paperback sticking from Roxanne's book bag.

"It's a friend's book," she explained, looking embarrassed as she pushed it back down.

"So let me see it," said Pat.

"No, it's private!" Roxanne told her.

Pat said, "You think I've never read something that I have no business reading?" She laughed.

"My mother would kill me if she saw this book," Roxanne confessed. "I may let you borrow it though. But I have to ask my friend whose sister it belongs to."

"I spoke to Mrs. Weisbaum, and I think I may have a regular baby-sitting job," Pat mentioned. "I'll find out today. I'll be so happy if I get it, so that I can buy me some things."

"I hope you get it," Roxanne said, thinking to herself how lucky she was. She had never hit-a-lick, or even thought about it! Everything she needed, her mother and father bought. She had a lot to be thankful for, she realized.

She was relieved to have the party off her conscience now. All that worrying had truly weighed her down! Margarita was probably right, she figured — when Margarita said that Marcus wouldn't want to have anything else to say to her after today. But this was okay. She was hoping it went this way. She wanted to have all her problems out of the way at once. The party. Marcus. *Everything!*

On her way to class, Roxanne walked behind Margarita, Laquita, and Shanika who were talking steadily about the party.

"Raheem's having it in the basement of his house," Margarita was explaining.

"It'll be the first time I've gone to someone's house who doesn't live in an apartment," said Shanika.

"I have an aunt who lives in a house in Queens," said Laquita. "And we go out there for cookouts sometimes. And another cousin of mine has a house in the East Bronx. It's nice up there."

"I didn't know *any* black people had houses in Riverdale," said Shanika.

"Oh, suuure," went Margarita. "A few. Raheem

says he lives more on the edge of Riverdale though. You know, down the hill, sorta."

Roxanne smiled to herself, as she turned in another direction. It would have been kind of interesting to see what Raheem's house looked like! The "edge" of Riverdale, where they had said he lived, was where her classmates Lisa and Jessica lived. They would both tell you that they were *from* Riverdale though! You'd better not try to tell them they were from any EDGE! she recalled, walking on and smiling to herself. All through elementary school, they said they lived in Riverdale, New York, to keep from saying the Bronx! I can't see putting the Bronx down all the time though. Some parts are rough. But so are parts of Manhattan, Brooklyn, and everywhere else! she concluded, walking on inside the classroom.

Pat had to go for her job interview at lunchtime. Before leaving, she went up and asked Roxanne, "Did you hear anything about some people cuttin' school today to go to a party?"

"You know?" Roxanne asked.

"Everybody's talking about it," she said.

"Yeah, I heard about it," Roxanne admitted. "A few people I know are going," she added without calling any names.

"They got a lot of nerve!" said Pat.

151

"Stupid nerve!" Roxanne emphasized, like she hadn't considered going herself. "I'm walking up to Angelo's," she told Pat.

"Oh, good!" she said."I'm going that way."

As they walked down the hallway, Roxanne saw Margarita and N.E. giving their books to a ninth-grader to put in his locker. It had to be a ninth-grader, because they were the only students with lockers. Riverdale Junior High had not been built to hold the number of students who had ended up there. So there weren't enough lockers to go around. The ninth-graders were the lucky ones to receive them. Everybody else had to carry their things all day. That is, unless they knew a ninth-grader.

Roxanne felt a little envious, realizing that Margarita and N.E. knew one now. But even that, she decided, wasn't worth the trouble they were risking.

She and Pat saw a lot of hustling and bustling as they left the building. Kids were whispering and giggling as they walked in what appeared to be the direction of the party.

When she and Pat split up, Roxanne walked into Angelo's prepared to eat alone. But she found Rolland there.

"Yo, Roxie!" he said, as she walked toward the pizza stand. "What's up? I just ordered. I would've asked you to come with me. But after getting turned down yesterday . . ."

"Oh, I would've said yes," she told him. "Who's left to eat with?" Roxanne laughed as she looked around the deserted pizza parlor. The place was usually packed. But hardly anyone was here today. She ordered a slice.

"Yeah, quite a few cut out," Rolland commented. "Let me pay for you," he said, taking out money.

"No, I got it," she said.

"No, let me," he insisted.

"Well, next time I pay for yours," Roxanne said, giving in. "You're spending your mama's money, the same as I'm spending mine!"

"True," he admitted with a smile.

"We're pretty lucky, you know?" she said.

"Yeah?" he asked, leading the way to a table. "How you figure?"

"Oh, just having money every day. Decent clothes, and all," she added, with thoughts of Pat still lingering.

"That's what we have parents for," said Rolland. "To give us what we need! Even though some don't!"

"And some can't," Roxanne added.

"I'm just glad to have at least *one* who does!" he stated.

"You know I actually thought a minute about going to that party," Roxanne said, switching the subject.

"CUTTIN'?" Rolland asked, so shocked that he

had to lay down his pizza for a minute.

"Uh-huh," she mumbled between bites. "I thought about it. I was going to do something that I really didn't want to do just because somebody else said I should . . ."

"I have to *really* want to do a thing to go 'long," said Rolland. "And sometimes it has to be two *really's*. I have to really, really want to do it! But if I can't come up with at least one really, I generally forget the whole thing! Now I *really really* would like to come study with you some evening," he said leaning across the table and making her laugh.

"Oh, *really*?" she came back with, never giving him an answer.

As they walked back to school, Roxanne felt even better now. It was good to know that she had done the right thing. She didn't even mind Rolland's endless chatter about her picking the right crowd to run with. Pat caught up with them before they reached the building.

"I got the job!" she shouted with excitement. "I got the job!"

"Super!" Roxanne shared her joy. "Rolland this is Pat. Pat, Rolland," she said afterwards, introducing the two.

"Hi," said Pat.

"Hi," Rolland responded.

Roxanne was glad that he didn't start walking fast and acting like he couldn't be seen with someone who wasn't black. Roxanne had come to learn that some kids were like that: Black ones who didn't want to be seen with anybody white. White ones who didn't want to be seen with anybody black. For some, it was okay in private just speaking one-to-one, but not in public when you were with your friends. Others weren't down for it privately or publicly. Roxanne had never discussed this subject with Rolland, so she was glad to see that he was cool. Rolland was even trying to look interested as Pat talked about the after-school job she'd landed. This was real decent of him, Roxanne thought.

Pat skipped up the school steps, saying that she'd see them later. This proved to Roxanne that it wasn't like Margarita and N.E. claimed. Pat knew what time it was! She was cool.

"I'll see you in a few minutes," Roxanne told her, staying behind with Rolland.

"See you after school maybe?" Rolland asked, reaching over and taking Roxanne's hand. When she didn't take it back right away, he added, "You letting me hold your hand?"

"At least I'm *outside* the building!" she remarked, laughing and snatching her hand away now. "Want to wait for me this afternoon?"

"Didn't I just ask you that?" he said.

"All right. See you later then," she added giggling.

"You all heard what happened?" Maxine asked, standing in front of the projects when Roxanne and Rolland got off the bus.

"No, what?" they asked at the same time.

"The police broke up this party in Riverdale this afternoon!" Maxine began. "And, girlfriend, I'm so glad to see you! Because soon as I heard . . ."

"What went down?" Rolland asked as he and Roxanne followed Maxine to a bench to sit.

"They got caught, that's what!" fired Maxine. "I heard it was like a marathon coming from the basement of the place! They say that the school principal was there, the police — and that they were taking names!"

"Oooh!" cried Roxanne, with her hand flying to her mouth. "I'm so glad I didn't go!" she said, shivering at the thought of how close she came to being a part of it all. "How did you find all this out, Max?"

"Boo, I mean Clarence told me," she explained. "He just ran upstairs for a minute. He said he almost went himself!" Maxine continued. "I told him, boy, you know better!"

Boobie returned now with his boom box, joining them on the bench with more details. According to him, it was the large crowd that drew attention. "Someone in the neighborhood must have called the cops," he said.

"Ooooh," said Roxanne.

"Clarence, you and Roxanne both crazy for ever entertaining goin' to that thing!" declared Maxine.

"Oh! You knew Roxie was thinking 'bout it, too, huh?" went Rolland. "Nobody tells me anything anymore."

"Oh, let it rest will ya Rolland?" Roxanne said laughing and pushing at him playfully. "You actin' like I went to the thing!"

"Y'all know Tank from building ten who never stops eating," said Boobie. "They say he was making hot dogs when the party got busted. Everybody was busy trying to run, and my man Tank was steady trying to grab his grub!" he ended, making them laugh.

"Wonder what about your friends?" asked Maxine.

"Oh yeeah." Roxanne sighed. "Even though they were dissin' me for not going, I still hate thinking of them getting caught. They might even get suspended behind this thing!"

"I heard the principal ain't big on suspending," said Boobie. "They say he likes to punish you elementary-style."

"What are you talkin' about?" Maxine asked, frowning.

"Must I always break everything down for you?" he shot back at Maxine.

"Not if you speak in halfway normal English!" she responded.

"Well, if you let me finish. All I was trying to say is that the principal punishes the same way that it was done in elementary school. Instead of sending kids home, like happens with my brother at Kennedy, Mr. Rubin punishes you at school with stupid stuff like we had at P.S. 9! Y'all remember: Getting sent to a corner! Or being told to write your name five hundred times. And junk like that!"

"I can't believe the man'll have junior high kids doing something so wack," stated Rolland.

"That's what they say," Boobie repeated.

"I thought we were getting away from all the kiddie stuff," Roxanne commented.

"Me, too," said Rolland. "But seem like a lot o' what be goin' down in junior high ain't much different from P.S. 9! Teachers still be on your case, giving you piles o' homework . . ."

"What y'all expect?" cried Maxine. "You're still in school! What you think junior high suppose to be? Like a country club?"

"I hear that's how it is where you at up the hill!" Clarence cracked.

"There you go again, Boobie. Talkin' what you don't know. When were you at my school?"

"I don't have to go there to know it's a jive school," he said.

"Jive how?" Maxine fired.

"Didn't you say they have a soccer team?"

"What has that got to do with anything?" Maxine questioned.

"Name a black soccer player!" he challenged her.

"Time out!" Roxanne shouted, holding up a hand. "I don't feel like refereeing this afternoon."

"Yeah. Me neither," Rolland kidded. "Why you wanna be puttin' her school down, man?"

"Maxine know I'm just playing," said Boobie. "She knows a day can't pass without me raggin' her school. I'm just stupid-jealous 'cause she's up there where I can't get a chance to see her every day."

"You see me every day, boy," she uttered.

"Yeah, but dudes up there got the edge all day at school."

"Shut up, Clarence," Maxine told him blushing.

Boobie and Maxine continued cracking jokes. But not at each other. There was plenty to joke around about school and different people in the hood. It felt like old times again to Roxanne, as she sat laughing at Maxine and Boobie holding court. She hadn't had this much fun in a while.

Boobie was speaking now about not liking his science teacher. "Yeah," he told them. "She's forcing everybody to come up with a project for this science fair, you know. And I can't see it. Some people interested in that sorta thing. And some ain't. So why she gotta force everybody to participate? I say she prejudice!"

"Just 'cause the lady say you got to do a project?" cried Maxine. "You need to stop!"

"Yeah," Roxanne interjected. "Some kids holler prejudice too much."

"Well, it's true a lot at school," Rolland stated.

"Yeah, but when you keep saying it every time you don't like something, it gets to be like the wolf story, you know? Nobody'll pay you any attention afterwhile," said Maxine. "Clarence, you were saying the same thing last week about your English teacher."

"Yeah, but that *was* prejudice," he insisted. "Check this out," he said turning to Rolland. "She come tellin' me out loud that I need to stop droppin' my g's when I speak. Ain't that cold?"

"Yeah!" Rolland agreed.

"Now I can see if she wanted to call me to the side," said Boobie. "But from how she did it, I don't even feel like saying nothin' in her class now! Everytime I open my mouth, I feel like I'm that commercial. You know, the one where everybody stops to listen!"

"My mother's always telling me to switch up my speech for school," said Roxanne.

"You hafta!" said Maxine. "Like I was trying to tell Boobie. It's like you be bilingual, you know?"

"Well, like I said," Clarence continued, "I wasn't saying she was prejudice for what she said, but how she did it! Dissin' me that way in a whole room of people just for soundin' different. That was prejudice!"

"But deep down, you know it's another story far as that science project goes, don't you?" Maxine pressed on.

"Weeelll," Boobie said, laughing.

"One thing I have to say is that in school 'n out, y'all don't be going through the same amount of prejudice as black guys," said Rolland.

"I don't know about all that!" fired Roxanne. "Kenya, this girl I knew was telling me about how she couldn't get pass a doorman right in Riverdale."

"And when I go into the deli up there at lunchtime," Maxine added, "you should see how they watch me! But I'm not studyin' 'bout them myself. Long as I have money, I go where I wanna."

"Still, Rolland's right," Boobie followed up with. "We get a harder way to go."

"Like y'all were sayin' that sometime we can't talk that talk. Well, we also can't walk that walk!" said Rolland.

"Wooord," added Boobie. "Course, sometime it makes no difference. You can have your hat on

161

straight. Your shoulders up. Be sounding like Prince Charles himself. And you *still* get looked at funny in a store."

"And white people not the only ones who be dissin' us that way either!" cried Rolland.

"Wooord." Boobie repeated.

"Nobody's saying there is no prejudice out here," said Roxanne. "You just can't be hollerin' it for every lil' thing."

"Like being told to do a science project!" snapped Maxine.

"I still say the lady got her pets," Boobie charged now.

"Yeah. And it's probably the ones who 're doing their science projects like they're supposed to," Maxine ended, laughing. "Me, I don't worry about who they like the best. I just always try to remember what I heard a teacher say to some kids who were actin' out in class one day. She told them, 'I've got mine; you've got yours to get!' So that's all I worry about. Getting mine!"

"I hear that!" Roxanne chimed.

Maxine's favorite song was on the box now. Turning up the volume, she pulled Boobie up from the bench. And the two began working out right there in front of the building.

"They're crazy!" Roxanne turned and said to Rolland as they watched Maxine and Boobie do the electric slide. The two glided back and forth on the concrete like they were on a dance floor.

"Come on," Maxine shouted, motioning for Roxanne and Rolland to join them. "Get busy, y'all!"

"Uh-uh," went Roxanne. "Two nuts in front of these projects is enough!"

Maxine and Boobie continued boogying until someone hollered out the window at them. It was Mrs. Edwards warning that if they didn't cut out the noise, she'd come downstairs and do it for them! Before Boobie could get back to his boom box, Roxanne had shut the music down. "I hope Mrs. Edwards couldn't tell from upstairs that I was part of the rowdy crew out here!" she told them, cracking up.

Roxanne stayed outside, enjoying her friends a while longer. She realized that it was getting late, and that she was missing her afternoon TV programs. But as she said to Rolland when finally heading inside, "Boobie and Maxine together, beat *Oprah* and *Donahue* any day!"

Marcus called later, and had the nerve to complain about Roxanne not *trying* to come to the party! "At least your friends showed up!" he said, like they hadn't all ended up in trouble for it! And he went from that to the movie business, asking if she thought she could go tomorrow night!

"No, I can't!" she shouted through the phone. "Why don't we forget it!"

"The movies?" he asked.

"Talking to one another," she indicated.

"You took the words out of my mouth," he said, trying to save face. "I was thinking the very same thing. Because like — like — " he struggled to finish. "Like, I like girls who 're a lil' less scary. So I'll just see you around school," he ended, sounding pretty weird to her.

" 'Bye," she said, happy to have this over with at last!

"I'm like you are now!" Roxanne told Rolland first thing Sunday morning. She was on her way to church, and he was coming from Burger King with his breakfast.

"Like me how?" he asked.

"Back in the world," she sang out.

Although she hadn't exactly expected to, Roxanne didn't hear from Margarita or N.E. all weekend about what happened at the party. It would have been much too cold though, she figured, to call them up and ask.

They're probably mad with me, and are going to come to school acting funny, she thought right up until Monday morning. But she had a big surprise waiting for her when she got to school!

When Roxanne walked into homeroom, she found Margarita sitting in back with Pat, talking away!

"I was waiting for you!" Margarita announced when she saw her. "I wanted to call you over the weekend, but I'm under punishment! The school called my house and everything, girl! I was already in hot water about my report card. And now this! My father says no more phone calls at all! I don't know what I'm going to do!"

"Maybe if you get a better card next round, he'll ease up," Roxanne suggested.

"I can hope 'n pray," she said. "I told Pat all about what happened. I couldn't wait for you. Laquita and Shanika are not speaking to me for getting them into trouble! This is the last time I'll try leaving school on the sly!"

"How do you think you all got caught?" Roxanne asked.

"I don't know. They say somebody 'roun' the way called the police. But N.E. said she thought it was a person who Raheem kicked out the party."

"Oh, yeah?" went Roxanne. "Over what?"

"Smoking. Raheem told people up front that he was allergic to cigarettes. So when the guy igged this, Raheem kicked him out. N.E. thinks he was the one. Maybe so. But then, it also could have been the man at the deli who called. Kids were running back and forth. Raheem had like some potato chips and a few corn doodles out. But you know some people. They got to eat. This one big joker started saying he wanted him some *real* food. So like he goes and buys frankfurters to cook! Then Raheem discovers there's no mustard in his house. So somebody else has to run back to the store for that. With all that runnin' in and out the house, it's no wonder we got caught!"

"So like where were you when the police came?" Roxanne asked, hungry for the real dirt.

"Girl, on the floor rockin' back!" Margarita stated. "And so was N.E. We had a line going. Guys on one side, girls on the other. And we were lookin' good, too. Just like on *Soul Train*!" Then next thing we know somebody comes flying through hollerin' *run*! The bright lights came on and I was out o' there!"

"Bright lights?" asked Roxanne.

"Oh, yes. Like there was these blue lights in the basement. Raheem had it hooked up!"

"Not quite hooked up enough though, huh?" Roxanne joked.

"I bet you all were scared!" said Pat.

"Honey, that ain't the word." Margarita sighed.

"Maybe you and N.E. will be down for my study group idea now," Roxanne suggested.

"Yeah, N.E.'s in trouble, too," Margarita reported. "N.E. say the only places she's allowed to go for the next six months are to school and church!"

"Those are the only places I normally go!" Pat cracked, making them laugh.

"I'm glad I changed my mind!" Roxanne let slip out.

"You mean you thought about going?" Pat asked with surprise.

"Yes, she *sure* did!" Margarita was quick to say.

"Ooouuu, Roxanne," Pat snapped on her, making a face. "I'm too scared o'you!" she ended, sounding all hip.

Roxanne smiled. It was as though they had come to the end of a game they'd been playing. Each of them had fronted in one way or another. Now everything was in the open. No one in their group had it all together, but then, who *did* in seventh grade? As far as she could tell, nobody. Black or white. From the projects or wherever, it was clear that the very coolest, could only be but so cool, the first year of junior high. So all that she, Margarita, Pat, or any of them could do was just keep going. And sooner or later, maybe they'd get it all together.